SEASON
AT
COOLE

SEASON

AT

COOLE

BY
MICHAEL STEPHENS

AN AFTERWORD

BY

THOMAS MC GONIGLE

THE DALKEY ARCHIVE PRESS

SEASON AT COOLE. Copyright©1972, 1984 by Michael Stephens.
AN AFTERWORD. Copyright©1984 by Thomas McGonigle.

All rights reserved under International and Pan American
   Copyright Conventions. Printed in the United States
   for The Review of Contemporary Fiction, Inc.

LIBRARY OF CONGRESS CATALOGING IN PUBLICATION DATA

Stephens, Michael
   Season at coole.
   I. Title
PS3569.T3855S4   1984   813'.45   84-21373
ISBN 0-916583-02-3
ISBN 0-916583-03-1

THE DALKEY ARCHIVE PRESS
1817 79th Avenue
Elmwood Park, IL 60635

FOR MORE AND THE FUTURE
AND OKHEE, PAST, PRESENT, & FUTURE

"All is not then yet quite irrevocably lost."

—Samuel Beckett

SEASON
AT
COOLE

CHAPTER ONE

The father—*God bless and expand him*—he was sitting
at the dining room table; he was scratching his head,
where the bald spot showed through like a new monk
tonsured. "The damn guineas on the docks," he said, to
no one particular, not sipping his beer either, but staring
it down, sempiternally. "The wacky kids, no presents, no
presents, no presents for any of them." The father (and
using the word loosely): "My own wife a wino." "My
own kids drug addicts." "The damn guineas, they're taking over the docks." *Allah be praised,* it was Christmas
time, that was certain, because a sudden hassidic gloom
had settled over Inspector Coole, the U.S. Customs official and father of nine plus, shall we say, children. He
scratched the tonsured-like spot at the back of his head,

bewildered, overcome with nostalgia for his garbage dump home, the dinner plates uncleared and unwashed in front of him, the empty beer bottles forming little opaque brown monuments, the imaginary gravesites of his children. "The Chief," as he was called, because that is what he called each one of his children, was fat, but not merry; heavy, but not round; dark, gout ridden, soaking his ingrown toenails in a salad bowl under the table, hemorrhoids itching up a fierce disorder about his potbottom, he was a King Midas of Shit, and he knew it better than the subjects he tried his despotism on; the beer in his belly felt lumped, like a small coal, about the rippling center of his belly button, sad, sad, sad Leland Coole.

Earlier at dinner:

"Pass the salt, Oona," Sam said.

The father started to rattle his plate at the head of the table, his eyes darting from child to child, their similar features causing his already queered head to consider his life a final hallucination of his past, he said:

"Keep the peas moving or leave the table, Terry," slapping one of the younger brothers on the head, like a vaudeville act except for the pained expression Terence's face had.

"Leave the table, Deirdre," mother Rose said, because D. spilt her milk onto Sam's new dress; Leland Jr. sulked in his meat, tearing pieces from his plate, ravenously, for this Christmas he and the old man had decided to go off the edge of the planet like a brace of ducks in orange sauce together, a duet for father and son, where usually poppa does it now at Christmas, his son Leland will do it a few weeks or months later. Leland, the oldest son, threw his plate across the table, letting the gravy ooze down the dirty blue wall like a wound, he said he was going to kill tonight if it didn't get quieter around here, and then deserted the dining room for his cellar, cursing.

"Fucking Irish savages, swamp dwellers, green niggers," fat Lee, he mumbled as he stumbled, as he descended the steps of the cellar as if into the lower reaches of Dante's Hell.

"You think Michael will come home tonight?" Terence asked.

The old man looked at him menacingly, for the boy Terry had mentioned the taboo name, he was talking about the profligate who was thrown out years ago.

"Yeah, when's Mickey Mack ever coming home?" Oona asked, breaking her silence of three months at the dinner table.

"Not another word or you don't get a thing for Christmas," The Chief said to the collected body before him, they were his wife and kids, but you would never know this had they not spoken, looked, and acted alike.

"It would be nice to see my third oldest son," mother Rose said, but the old man cut her off, saying:

"If I find that bottle of vodka you hid, I'll break it over your head."

That's a lie! There must be a lighter side.

Fiat lux:

"Is Leland going into the hospital again for his head?" Deirdre asked her mother, and the father broke in.

"Not another word about that maniac or I'll have you all locked up tonight!"

"She only asked a simple question," Sam said.

The father got up, pulled off his belt, his pants falling

down, he held them up in one hand, as he chased his oldest daughter around the table, finally giving up the fourth time around, and instead slapped Terry, who was laughing.

"Exposing himself in front of his mother, a disgrace, a nuisance, and there's no excuse for Leland's behavior."

They agreed or not, the girls clearing part of the table, but their father chasing them away when half done, Oona and Sam went up to the head room for weed, Terence and Wolfe to mess around in the attic of this scroungy house the family dwells in on Long Island, Irish beggars surrounded by the tacky elegance of newly rich, almost rich, and the rich; they had roosted in this run down house for the last twenty-five years, since they left Brooklyn, but never poor enough or humble to collect welfare, The Chief made it to work every day for the preceding two decades on the docks, check your bags and arrest you for contraband the minute you step off the boat onto the fatherland soil, for instance, "I knew Michael had drugs on him when he got off the ship from Morocco," he said, and his house was run accordingly, as long as he could stay drunk enough to endure the noise, the nine plus children he created so that he could name his suburban house Bedlam.

Oona was back downstairs after a few tokes off the hash pipe and cleared the remaining plates into the kitchen, soaking them in hot water, but not washing them, she'd let them sit there for a few days until the pile was larger than herself and the spirit moved her toward this task. She'd then dive in, soaping down the muck off the plates, and stacking them in a cupboard next to a paint can or a motorcycle engine part or broken toaster or bicycle part, logic had failed these people years ago, and if the mother Rose had her way, the dishes would have been put in the garage with the lawn mower, where dishes belonged, she said, "because that way we wouldn't use them as often as we do," and placing clean under-wear and socks in a closet in the kitchen too, she held a rosary in one hand, praying for her family, the Hail Marys mumbled under her breath inaudibly, occasion-ally scratching her crotch or armpit, smiling at her daughter and thinking about her stash in the basement, which she would have to sneak past Leland, lock the laundry room door, and then imbibe until she was again a Queen as she thought herself should be in these trying times. Glassy eyed, she snuck past Leland, who was rip-ping books in his corner of the cellar, drinking his bour-bon, and cursing the woman, who he did not see sneak past him to her laundry room, but whose presence he felt, he said, "like the fifth wound in Jesus' side, fuck them all!"

Mother Rose plopped on the laundry she was to wash, already high and wanting to go higher, she opened the vodka bottle first, drank a good swill and washed that down with a nip from the muscatel bottle, she was talk-ing out loud, but not loud enough for her son, the other side of the cellar partition, to hear. Her dress was akimbo past her thighs, the buttons opened at the top, her hair kinky and uncombed, her smell pungently al-coholic and lonely, whimpering, whispering, holding court with the Virgin Mary, who she often saw and spoke with, while drunk in her part of the cellar.

"Then my mother had a maid, so I never really knew how to do a wash properly, and she made the beds too.

There was a cook for dinner, and my father owned these beautiful carriages and horses on his father's estate on Long Island. We were related to the Barrymores and my mother went to the best boarding schools in the East, she raised me to respect you, Mary in Heaven, varoom! as fine as a new Dodge station wagon, this is your child Rose talking to you from the cellar. Do you think when I die, they'll set up a grotto down here, perhaps miracles, just one miracle and we'd be fine for life. I'm serious, I don't want to be a saint, but the children might like the attention. Oh, I'm not making any sense tonight, I'm drunk, I'm drunk, Mary Button of Barusalem. Shit! Oops, I never used to curse, shit! I never used to, Virgin, you know this by me. Love me once more tonight, Mother of God, goddamn, old titbags Mary Glue, how are you? I'm fine, and you? All right. I can't stand it, I can't, let me die now, they'd give me such a fine funeral, honest, they love me up there, I'm loved like crazy, by all of them, all good children, famous, grownup, holy, they go to church every Sunday, and even if they don't, they tell me they do, which makes me feel better, right?

"I don't care if any of my children ever work, I'm a beatnik, I am, Mary, you know this. This is a commune and I am Queen of the Communists; I used to work for a wealthy socialist family in Sands Point, when we lost our money, and I became a nurse. They were fine people, Jewish, and respectable too. We must love everyone, the Jews, the Italians on the docks, the colored, the butcher, little trees, balloons, clouds and rain. See, I'm a poet like my son Mickey Mack, and he thought it all came from the Coole side of the family. I'm not making sense, so I don't care if the children ever work, but if they do, ten percent should go to their mother and father, right or wrong, there's no excuse if they don't give us some money if they're working, right? We raised them, and they owe it to us. Twenty percent, if they live at home, like Leland, and they're grown up, over eighteen years old, and not in the Army. None of my sons have to go to war, if they don't want to, I believe this Mary from Jesus, your son."

Leland walked into the laundry room.

"Drunk again and talking to Mary, eh?"

She is stunned.

"Oh, Leland, you scared me."

"I scare you, eh?"

"Yes, you do, I mean, you did."

"Well, fuck you, Rosey. Fuck you, Jesus, Mary, and your family upstairs," he said, swigging off her wine bottle, and walking out with the bottle.

She lay on the laundry.

"Thank god he didn't get the vodka," she said, pulling it out of a pair of heart printed boxer shorts.

"Poo poo stains," she said, holding the shorts up, then throwing them in the corner.

She held her rosary beads in one hand and the vodka bottle in the other. Mother Rose returned to the Virgin, as though nothing had happened.

"Never been a good cook and the beds never get made, but I do make a meal whenever anyone wants it, and the children never go unclothed or starved, that's the important thing. There's no excuse not to feed them and to give them clothes, I always say. Rose Kennedy, you know what it's like to raise a big family, I know you understand. I cook an average of twenty-three meals a day,

I figured it out recently. Oh, Virgin Mary Shoe, there are holes in my sneakers, and I'm too lazy to go to the store three blocks away for a new pair, I haven't worn high heels since the funeral Leland and I went to for his stepmother five or six years ago, maybe ten years ago, longer, yes much longer than that. The *Daily News* and a glass of wine are my only pleasures in the day time, and at night, I sometimes can come down here to pray and drink in peace. You tell me how we each have our special cross to bear in life, like your son Jesus Boots, all I want to know, why so many? One would do fine, a retarded son or a deaf daughter, but they're all so healthy when they grow up, they don't need me to take care of them, they don't want me anymore to sit up all night to hug and kiss them out of a nightmare, except maybe Wolfe, my youngest, my precious baby, my little Communist baseball hat."

"Pull yourself together," she hears, thinking it the Virgin talking to her, it is her son Leland, calling at the other end of the cellar, he is talking with himself and has forgotten that he's seen this apparition of his mother Rose a few moments earlier.

"Yes, I must do that. Look! I've pissed all over the laundry. Thank goodness I wasn't wearing underwear, I'm tired, I'm so tired. Give me one excuse Mary, so I won't have to confess again that I'm drunk. I love my children, my little crosses in life. Oh, pray for your little shitbag Rose, Virgin, and I'll raise my Communists, share and share alike, one for all and all for nothing, but not a word of this to their father. I should die before he found out I'm this way in Purgatory . . ."

The rosary bead raced faster through her hand and

the vodka bottle was tipped for its last drops. Rose lay in the dirty pile of laundry, and she cried.

Oona was walking through the living room bound upstairs to the head room again, when the phone rang, she went to answer it, because it might be one of her boyfriends. The old man was running to grab the phone out of her hand, he plowed through the room like a hippo after a nature photographer, a wild boar stalking meat, Black Irish Coole was grabbing the phone out of his daughter's hand, the receiver went dead, his black eyes like a predatory bird, his long beaked nose, the curly black hair, except for the bald spot in the back, his body was a pear, and rising up and down from the excursion, like a bellows, the belly hanging over the belt of his pants, the cuffs dragging along the floor, hobbling from one foot to the other to keep the weight off the ingrown toenail on his right foot, and then keeping the weight off the ingrown toenail on his left foot, he tripped over his cuffs and was entangled in the phone wire, frantically trying to extract himself from this condition.

He began to rip the phone out of the wall.

"No more phone calls, I've had it with that damn thing, do you hear me, Oona, I've had it, I've had it, do you hear," he said, either enjoying the repetition or unaware of it, the Inspector repeated himself again. "I've had it, I've had it, do you hear me, Oona." But she wasn't listening, going into the kitchen for an Oreo, her next stop was upstairs to her older sister Sam (her real name was Sandra, though she wound up being called Sam, another one of the boys, she was the fourth child, first daughter on the right, another dark one from the father's side).

When the phone rang again, he got out of his chair, to rip it out of the wall.

"I'm going to have this thing taken out," he said to Oona, meaning he was going to tear it out of the wall.

"It's been nothing but trouble since they put it in. You kids don't know the luxuries I give you. There's no excuse for this phone here."

Oona rushed to the phone before him, but the call was for her daddy.

"It's for you," handing him the receiver, he hung it up, and started to pull on the cord again, but his strength, which he had, was not with him tonight.

"I don't care who it's for, this goddamn thing has got to go."

Oona, half his size, a miniature in a family whose members were mostly half the size of other people, she was under five feet tall, she walked to the other side of the room, sat down in a chair, and told him:

"It was the police."

But he continued with the cord, straining, turning blue, unable to unhinge this evil communications system from the wall. The phone rang again. The Chief finally registered his daughter's message, and being who he was at the time of the year he was in, as Sam said earlier, "daddy gets his period once a year and for two weeks before Christmas his blood drips everywhere," he held the receiver, not answering yet, for he expected the worst, and seizing on the picture of his children at the dinner table earlier, the Inspector was trying to figure who wasn't there and might be in trouble. These sons, he

20

thought, what a cross to bear, what a pain in the ass worse than the guineas on the docks and the wacky government he worked for, though he couldn't remember who was missing, since he couldn't remember any of their names at that moment, simply thinking to himself, "one of the chiefs must be in trouble." The phone kept ringing, ringing. Inspector Coole paused, looked impishly at his daughter, his teeth never showing, he looked about fifteen years old, pausing to let the phone ring again, and turning to Oona, he said: "It must be for me." "I'm tired of this," she said, imitating her father, "answer the phone." "Now don't get wacky with me, Oona," he said, trying to stall his responsibility with the phone, for he never got phone calls at home and occasionally received them at the pier, and he was worried, which chief was in trouble, and what were their real names, he thought? What were their names?

He picked up the receiver.

"Hello, Coole residence."

In his most pleasant voice.

The voice at the other end of the phone could be heard screaming.

"I don't care whose residence it is, put your father on the phone."

Pausing, again, he attempted to recover his composure, no, he never had that. He paused to get his breath in anticipation of the worst, which son would it be? The big chief, the other one, the dark one, what's his name, which one?

"This is him, er, hello, this is the head of the, er, this is Mr. Coole."

Well, he had better get his ass into the city, because

they got a relative of his going to be locked up in the nut ward. This is what the Inspector heard:

"Your son Michael went crazy and would you please come to Manhattan or we'll have to take him to Belle-vue."

But what he heard and what the police said, well, the police said:

"We have a relative of yours and would you please come to Manhattan or we'll have to take *her* to Belle-vue."

But since all his daughters and his wife were at home, it had to mean a son, a *him* and not a *her*, and Michael Mack as opposed to Emmett, who the old man knew to be coming home that evening, it wasn't him, nor Patrick, who was in enough trouble with a grand larceny not to be foolish enough to get arrested for madness. It was Michael, he thought with the glow of inner logic on the old man's face now. The waiting chief was Mackool, and after all these years, the third son was wigged out weirdie from drugs and poetry, and with initial fatherly pride, because he finally knew where his missing son was, the Inspector erupted into his usual hysteria.

"The chief's in Bellevue," he said to Oona.

"Which one?" she asked.

He hung up the phone, and without finding out the full details, but having automatically written down the address the police gave him, he was a nervous wreck, The Chief, running around the table three times before he got his directions and headed for the closet and his coat, pushing chairs out of his way, and resetting them in his way again, only to push them out of his way again as

22

he made a return trip through that passage, he ran out the door, and Oona heard him start the car, watched the car drive fifteen feet, back up, turn off the lights, turn off the engine, and come running back into the house, because he forgot to put shoes on.

"Which chief," Oona screamed.

He stopped short, reversing the left shoe to his right foot, and vice versa, he corrected this, and tripped on his cuffs.

"Michael's in Bellevue."

Oona looked at him with disbelief.

The Inspector looked back at her in amazement that he had discovered the right name, he thought, though wrong again, it was definitely a her, or to be more accurate, two hers, the old man's two half sisters, the twins Quif and Quim, rather Nora Eileen and Eileen Nora, who the old man hadn't seen in twelve or thirteen years, and since they were his only relatives left, after his mother died, his father died, and his step sister Aunt Augusta, then his stepmother, the only relatives he could think of, when the police explained to him on the phone, was a son, a chief, a boy named Mickey Mack Coole, since all the others were accounted for, and Quif and Quim, rather Nora Eileen and Eileen Nora, though the children—Jesus rest their happy souls—called his red-headed half sisters Quif and Quim, a more accurate name considering their looks; it had gotten so that whenever one of the chiefs referred to them as this, for instance, "whatever happened to Quif and Quim," Emmett asked? the father almost called them that too, but usually caught himself on the first one's name, Quif, and swore he'd break the child's neck who ever used that word again, when they talked about his beloved and insane half sisters.

"Michael?" Oona said.

The old man ran through the dining room, rearranged the chairs, cleared off some beer bottles from the table, tripped on his shoelace this time, laced them, tripped on his cuff, and mumbled his way out the door.

"Michael . . . Mickey Mack . . . god, he took too many drugs, I know that's what it was, Michael . . . out . . . got to go . . . Bellevue!"

Season's greetings came in the form of a telephone call from the police department, a fifteen cent call from Manhattan to Long Island, the old man was impressed, "that's the way the gov'mint should run things, they got the courtesy to notify me about my son," still thinking it was Mackool who wigged out in a tenement from poetry and dope. My son should have read less, he says, as he gets on his coat finally, the right arm in the right sleeve, he trips on the trouser cuffs again, looking to hit one of the kids for his own malfunctioning, they scatter, but impressed nonetheless with the Wheels of Justice, legal commerce speeds on, it was assuring for his gov'mint mind to know that other branches were as efficient as he thought his own was, and almost glad under his surface worries, because he was to have the phone taken out of the house two days earlier, saying:

"I must break communication with the enemy."

"Do you mean Oona?" Terry asked.

"No back talk, Terry, you know who I mean."

The enemy was his second daughter who smoked weed in her room, chanted, danced like a diva nude in moonlight through her head room, and because of these habits, the father was convinced she was out to get him, he'd swear out the warrants for his children's arrests; though now, here, in the dilapidated living room with a television set they acquired after fifteen years without one, he thought that would have to go tomorrow too. It was either the television or the telephone, and he would not live in a house with both items. The phone tonight was a good outside line to the world, and Inspector Coole could not help but be amazed by Progress, and so before he went out the door, with his arms in the right sleeves of his overcoat, his shoes on the right feet, a fedora on his head, he punched with his fist a hole through the television tube, as a toothpaste commercial blasted teeth and smiles and good American ways that in some subversive way Inspector Coole knew himself revolutionary under his skin, for he hated this country and its ways as much as his radical sons and daughters, and as he removed his fist from the hole in the television set, he said to Oona:

"I don't know what I'd do without a phone."

The car jerked, faltered, then slipped away on the icy street toward Manhattan and his duties as a father come to save a son he vowed his hatred for too many times to number. As he drove, images of his youth flashed through his head about MacDougal Street, Brooklyn, where he reeled out his childhood on the stoop outside his father's apartment house. His Irish momma dead in her grave at an early age, but his father the taxi driver who looked like Jack MacGowran the actor, the old

25

man's old man married this low rung lace curtain lady, who was later to teach Michael, Sam, and Emmett how to curse in Irish as she stuck her fat ass out the first floor window to the banana man in his horse drawn cart, though the Inspector never was to learn of these capers, when his children went to visit his stepmother in Brooklyn for a vacation. He thought of the stoop, then about the boarding house he lived in in Washington D.C., and how they were the happiest days of his life, homefries for breakfast, lunch, and supper; steaks on Saturday, fish on Friday from a newspaper, his bedroom lined and piled with empty beer bottles that he would make a fortune on, when he returned them to the store for the deposit money; onions and mustard were on his mind; cheeses that stunk his room out, and dreams that he would one day become the American ambassador to Ireland, and he would have, he thought, had he not met that woman, Rose of Coole, who married him and never stopped having babies, never left him alone when he came home drunk or sober, and who insisted he was a bad father, when he knew for certain, it was she who was the bad mother.

When his father remarried, the Inspector acquired a step sister Augusta, his age, redheaded, fierce, and uncontrollable. Within a few years came Eileen and Nora (Quif and Quim), the old gal boozing and cursing her way through these once quiet railroad flat rooms, and spending his daddy's money like they won the Sweepstakes, they were broke and she was pregnant, and to make things worse, she had these redheaded twins, all redheads except for the old man and his old man, they were Black Irish, though when they grew up, Leland

26

Coole Sr. thought Eileen (Quif) was carrying the Moors invasion of Ireland too far the day she walked into his home on Long Island with her husband Jorge Carlos Panaqua, The Latin, he was euphemistically referred to, being a black Puerto Rican, who fathered a pretty black baby named Consuela Siobhan for Quif, rather Eileen, and her half brother, the Inspector was heard saying:

"She married a nigger is what she did!"

While his wife Rose Coole told him that Jorge Carlos was not colored but Spanish from Spain, which made it worse for her husband.

"That wacky Quif," he said, forgetting her real name. "That bum's a Portaricken nigger!"

And then there was Nora, the other half, unmarried, virginal, afraid to venture from the apartment for fear the blacks might rape her hide, and rather than a counterpart to her sister, she stayed her shadow and constant tormentor, though what their brother Leland did not know, since he had not heard from them in twelve years or more, he thought they were dead in their separate potter's field graves, and not living together in an apartment under the Williamsburg Bridge, for they never got along. But they did manage to live with each other, and had become so closely attached to themselves, that when the police phoned their brother Leland, it was impossible to put this dilemma in the plural, since it was difficult to say where Quif began and Quim picked up, where Eileen Nora's flesh ended and Nora Eileen's began.

The first thing to be understood about their brother Leland was, the Inspector never divulged his past, so the children had to fill in about his half sisters, and no matter how much the children or his wife asked about these

27

ladies, or what his father was like, how the twins Quif and Quim, two homely redheads straight from a Dublin nightmare, hollow cheeked and rotten teeth, they were the dregs of Irish potatoes in their cotton dresses, the maladroit skull Inspector Coole lived in found it hard to admit a relation to these things that haunted his childhood with their screams and taunts; the Inspector did not know that after his stepmother died and the will went entirely to Jorge Carlos through legerdemain, the father thought, that Nora Eileen (Quim) got caught in a fire in the basement and was in the hospital with her skin singed from her body an entire year, and that Jorge Carlos with his wife Quif and daughter Consuela Siobhan, bought the abandoned apartment building under the Williamsburg Bridge and moved his entire family plus a burnt out burnt up sister twin in the apartment on the first floor, only to o.d. six months prior to the Inspector's visit to Manhattan, where he expected to find his son Mickey Mack Coole and was instead to find his half sisters in demise, Consuela Siobhan dead several years earlier, when she fell into the river and was never found again, Jorge Carlos and Quif never reported the loss and continued to grovel in their digs under the bridge, and one almost understood their brother's reticence, why he didn't like to say how he came to be related to these princesses.

But Rose Coole could be depended on to reveal that horrible past with a clarity that made you think she relished the trials the father's ancestry had put him through when she said, "he doesn't like Christmas because their tree caught fire when he was a boy, and the building burnt to the ground." Simply stated, and almost under-

28

standable to the children's minds, as they watched the neighbors put up their wreathes, decorations, and colored lights around the front doors, all nine plus children cringed, collectively, knowing that Charles Dickens made Scrooge out so that all his humbugs finally brought home the goose, Merry Christmas One and All, Coole Tidings, hide from this Yule Blast, shove your Noël up the nearest reindeer's, what? The Inspector is escaping and must be brought back. He was driving in his Dodge station wagon and he was thinking about these things, though not suspecting that the party he was about to meet was Quif and Quim, his half sisters Eileen and Nora. You could smell the old man burning in his skull like a log on a fire the terrors that came down to him from this season.

What happened to Quif and Quim could have happened to anyone, if their last name were Coole, a.k.a. Panaqua, they flipped out.

The nice sized house under the Williamsburg Bridge was not cleaned in four years, shit on the floor and walls, they were found in a lake of piss, cuddled to one another, they found each the last animate objects that no longer assaulted them, welfare workers bitching they were too far gone for help, Quim at least had her excuse, with her skin pink from third degree burns she got while watching the pretty flames from the fire in the furnace on MacDougal Street, the cotton dress going up in seconds, but her red hair and skin taking longer, though no one in the MacDougal Street apartment paid much attention to her screams, because she did that nightly, saints trying to rape her in her sleep, Christ floating through her bedroom with a sheet over his head, later to be identified as Aunt Augusta drunk.

"They've come to get us," Nora said to Eileen.

This time, after several thousand predictions, she was right. They had come to get her.

Quif and Quim looked so happy to see their brother Leland.

The Inspector, shall we say, shit a brick, shit in his pants, dropped a load.

"Quif and Quim!" he said, not realizing it was the first time he had used the names his children so rudely tacked onto his half sisters.

"Leland!"

He was about to run over and hug them, then caught himself, when he caught a whiff of their smell, then realized they had not spoken to him in twelve years, when they could have, and right then, with the disappointment that his third son was still loose in the world untouched by the police and authorities, he took out his anger on these ladies.

The Inspector turned to the policeman.

"Lock them up, that's where they belong."

The cop equally annoyed, because he had to stay in the fetid room to fill out a report, but the old man saved the day with—

"There's nothing worse than Irish shit, let's take care of this in the bar across the way."

Where is that damn Mickey, he thought.

"Excuse me," the cop said.

"Nothing, let's get this over with and have a drink."

They adjourned to the bar, Quif and Quim off in an

ambulance bound for a glue factory, their reunion with their brother short lived, Quim was saying to Quif as they got into the ambulance, an orderly trying to guide them (a hulking eighty pounds each) in the back door without touching them much, it was impossible, though he had bloodier cases, this was the smelliest, their red hair smeared in brown feces and their orangey eyes staring no place particular, Nora was saying:

"Leland's good about taking care of us."

They nodded to each other, like toy rag dolls.

Leland was good. He was talking to the cop.

"There's no excuse for the way they behave."

The cop drank his drink.

"It sounds like you don't like your sisters."

"I love them as though they were my own children," he said, finishing his beer. "I wish them both a short and happy life."

CHAPTER TWO

Leland Jr. spraddles the toilet backward, watching a piece of shit in the bowl drydocked on the porcelain, he is in the cellar bathroom, watching this phenomenon, his turd is hung inches before the yellow pissy colored water. "It is like a brown whale washed up on the shore," he says outloud, but speaking to himself, Leland's life on the toilet is the only life he has, and if you didn't know Lee, you'd say his life was filled with, but listen, he got fired from a job in a plastic factory yesterday, and it's Christmas. Before that it was a steel mill and before that one a wheel factory, always factories, Trotsky, because that's where the oldest brother winds up drunk and lonely in towns that no one knows him in; Lee's notice-able immediately as "the new fat guy on the bearing machine," though if he were talking, he'd say, "I can't talk about this like that hotshit Mickey Mack Coole, he still won't admit that I taught him everything he knows about writing, the first one to turn him on to writing, I'll get to him later, let him rot in jail or wherever he is, like I did."

Lying in the cellar, Lee hears the children fighting upstairs, and pretty soon Leland will get up, wobbly, because he'd been drinking all weekend, three bottles of bourbon, slam one of those kids, because it's more than just not liking noise, he doesn't like children, and children who are related to him, he likes even worse, Leland hates god, his mother, and especially his country, and Leland would be a culture hero if he wasn't so fat, filthy, tired.

There are three hundred pounds of him now, and maybe next year four, because he grows with rage, and the wider it grows the fatter he gets, though you should realize, forget all that crap you have in your head, for where he really is is beyond hatred and further than despair, murder is around the corner, and if he had more courage he'd slash his throat, but suicides fail too, he can tell you about his one attempt, but right now, what he does have are two things to distinguish him from the other members of Coole; he is a great swimmer and has good teeth, the latter being near to a miracle considering the shitty Irish blood floating in their veins, alcohol offsets it all, that damn religion thrown into him, Leland created it himself, he'll tell you, the minute you ask why he's jammed in his head, he'll volunteer all information.

Instead of going to public high school after getting out of Saint Christopher's, his friend Charlie and the others went to Chaminade, good Catholic prep school in Mineola, a fine football team, kids think Leland a football player until he tells them differently, he hates the game, can't stand those American sports, and even the European ones, they stink too, except maybe bullfighting, but he don't know a thing about that either, it's just that Hemingway, "do I ever look like the young Poppa, lose a hundred pounds, people'd mistake me for his ghost or at least his son," he'd say, but way off, hold on mister, he says, you push me one more time, I'll knock those pearls in your mouth down your throat, Leland says to a shadow in the cellar, bad mood he's in, drinking, lying in bed all weekend, Christmas is an awful season, and drinking is all he's good for, even his mind trails off, he can't keep a coherent thought, it didn't used to be like that before Florida.

Fuck!

Just the name of that state pisses him off and those fucking kids screaming upstairs, he'll cut their throats, no, he won't yes, if he could only get out of this rotten bed, this cellar so damp, his bones ache and he's only twenty-seven years old, maybe twenty-eight, who keeps track anymore, what's it matter?

What was he talking about?

Cocaine nosed men with their nostrils drooped to their chests and spread there like nipples, Sex! Wipe it out, here he is again, adipose and shit in his socks, flab over his knee caps, triple chinned, honest to god female tits on his chest, and a belly covered with fur, rippled and rolling, fat pleating into stretch marks, stretch marks X'd over with another pocket of skin, multi-bellied he is; he's talking about high school, let Lee trace that thought; he

34

vaguely remembers what he was saying, shit. What he was saying was, all his friends went off to Catholic high schools, all of them intelligent but him, EL GORDO STU-PIDO, the fat one, Mr. Stupid, though he was thin then, and likable, he was the most liked guy, they loved him, the guys the girls the mothers of the girls, he could make a leper ring his bell with laughter, always a joke, and singing, the fucking Irish bit, a jig for Mary O'Hairy, that kind of thing, holy moly, he went to the rectory to speak with them about going to high school, this is what they said. There was a shortage of priests, so they got him enrolled in this high school in Brooklyn for boys who wanted to be diocesan priests, it was Cathedral Prep, and none of them fussy, they took Lee into the fold, so come the fall, take the LIRR into Brooklyn, get off at Atlantic Avenue, he's standing out on the subway "el" with his trench coat on, his hair slicked back, the coons in the station thought Leland a pimp or a pusher, never a young boy in the novitiate, studying to be a priest.

If they let him stay, he'd be a priest today, and not sure which would have been worse, that religious lie or his brain frizzy from Florida therapy sessions, they flunked him out, the bastards, all those great handball games in the school yard during lunch hour, all those great guys with five minute long Italian names from the Bronx, all priests now, and Leland Coole, here, foreign to earth once more, he thinks of jerking off, but the thought of touching that vestigial organ drives him to open the fourth bottle of bourbon, still not fucked, de-frocked, and loony.

He even has papers to prove his insanity.

Honorable nut case discharge from the Army, papers

from Florida, a few from Bellevue, Creedmore, West Islip, Rockland County, Kings County, if they were diplomas, he'd have a doctorate from every ivy league college in the country, but as it turns out, he doesn't have a high school slip because he failed shop course, Papers! He burnt and ripped up his wallet last night, who needs that name they stuck on him, like a Jew with a star on his forehead in Auschwitz, he's too fat for one short Irish name to fit him, Lee needs a long Russian Jew's name, a Cossack's head on the end of his sword; but unfucked, the prick shrivels from non-use, and with all that fat it looks like he has a cunt, he fucks himself.

His thoughts are hazy again, what he remembers starting to talk to himself in the mirror about was his teeth.

They're perfect, bucked, never a cavity in his life, he carries a toothbrush around with him in one pocket, a bottle of bourbon in the other. His parents both have their mouths filled up with false teeth, Leland thinks it's disgusting the way they take them out at night before they sleep, he's seen them in jars, those teeth, nights when he was slipping off the edge of the planet, he spoke with his parents' teeth, watching the white objects chatter back at him in the plastic glasses they were ensconced in, Fuck You, Leland, the big set said, horsey and indifferent to his swollen schizzy eyes, they said that he was a disgrace to the family, an embarrassment to the neighbors when he ran through the yard insane, raving about the final apocalypse, the horse teeth told him, you are a boob, Lee, a loony banana, a fruitcake, a weird fat man with a shriveled dick that's only good to let piss come out of the hole, your semen comes out cold, sterile, the chromosomes filled with mistakes from bad cross breeding, you are lucky not to fuck, for your children would be deranged, wicked, unacceptable to the community, you are the first and last outcast of Coole, you are the fatman, the lost one, the hopeless. The other set of false teeth in the jar smiled, my son, my son. His mother's false teeth made him jittery, because after all his bouts in this house, that woman remained Christian, not her really, but those teeth that he stared at in the night, they were understanding, sympathetic, forgiving, chipped and smiling, he hated them, the teeth of woman, bite your cock off, Lee, bite bite, he thought.

Mother Rose's teeth were the ones to stab into Lee, the mandibles gnawing the heavy flesh he carried to hide out in, it was a bad defense, he was not the armadillo, but instead, a flabby warrior home from his battles, he stared at those teeth, feeling superior to his creators, because he never had a cavity in his life, he held both sets in his hands the day before, it was just before dawn, the house quiet, uncomfortably so, because it harbored noise, it was an asylum for ranting, the quiet was a threat, as he stood there, loosed brain once again, his yearly ritual, he stared at these sets of teeth, letting them fly through the air like monkeys with wings, he wrapped up his mother's teeth in a towel, placing two buttons above the terrycloth mouth he made for teeth, she was all women, all woman, the supreme bitch, he held in his left hand, he carried out the acts of hari-kari, kamikaze, almost kissing the doll he made, but shrinking away at the last minute, he went whimpering to his cellar, medieval, in his perversions, the guilt that weighted him down, this flesh, he thought, as he opened his first bourbon bottle, is the price of my sins, damn the mother, he said, I salute thee father, fuck the children, I shall rule supreme, he said, letting the bourbon take him to the Middle Ages, by the time the sun rose Leland was Marlowe, awaiting a fatal knife in his gut, he wasn't down about it, for he had left a legacy of his writing, as he let the right hand sweep the panorama of the cellar, the papers, notebooks, paperbacks (he was thinking at this minute that he had written each one of them under a pseudonym, his *nom de guerre,* Henry Fielding), it was fine and proper, he felt, to be leaving this corporal world for an absolute spiritual realm, where his hate reached its apex, spiraling out of the cocoon of his fat body into the majesty of the cosmo All, his human defeat would be translated into an eternal love, he thought, as he stared, tranced, though menacing at this stage of his flip out, at the cover of a John Coltrane album, "A Love Supreme" . . .

Teeth were still with Leland by morning, he was thinking of his mother Rosey O'Coole, the first day she had her false teeth, she gets drunk and falls down the stairs, she chips the front one, though at least they look realer with that mar, Lee says to the floor, the old man's mouth is like a prune when he takes his out, particularly when he's drunk, god it's disgusting, he says, this human race, as he gropes in the dark for his bottle, then his pair of dungarees, he pulls the string on the fluorescent light, but it breaks, he's cursing, posting his rage upon the house all day until the evening when Deirdre walks down into the basement to tell him about Michael, he keeps saying, that bastard that bastard, till it becomes a Hindu chant, he stares at the beams in the ceiling, watching the beams buckle as the children run across them, let them fall in, he says, I dare them to fall in.

It would take an encyclopedia of filth and perdition to fill with the things he despises, and he'd be the first entry in the book, the first A for the biggest Asshole, he decides, as he mopes about his cellar, the dungeon, he is back to an atavistic source by afternoon, letting his elephant body ooze through the primal cellar air, damp and clustered with the demons of his life, he says, if you listened and stopped being afraid of him, you'd remember what he said, that he wasn't always fat, despicable, primordial in his hole getting mildewed, drunk by the boiler in lieu of the judgment, those kids upstairs, he'll wring one of their necks any second, they have no respect for their elders, Lee feels the carnivore leap from him, talk to him as he stares into the downstairs mirror, his heart pumps, he palpates his chest, still alive, damnit, he goes back to his mattress minus sheets for the last few months, he is assuming the role of the carminative man, dashing, farting, shitting in his pants, but thinking still, his brain tumbles, it refused to stop pumping despair through his body, Leland is too smart for his fat, his mind whips through thoughts, illogically, with the precision of a bone thin man in a cave with the ten great books of the Western World, he's trying to name them, but he can't get past his own name.

The Last Journey by Leland Coole.

Slush by Leland Coole.

Slime by Leland Coole.

Urine by Leland Coole, the last three being the trilogy, *The Corpulent Priest,* he runs down titles all day, night, mornings when he worked on machines in the shop before he was fired; titles come easy to him, the rage fits, he has the command of the language; he's spitting at his face in the mirror now, smearing the saliva over the image of himself, Bunny Berigan runs through his head, not really him, he's hearing Charlie Mingus do a version of "I Can't Get Started," it has become Leland's theme song, as he unglues his feet from the bathroom floor, walks back to his bed, that piss and jism stained mattress circa 1923, straw insides; the room smells of death, no, he wishes it would, it smells of the living in decay, a family with no bearings, Leland says it out loud, "these kids have no respect for their elders," feeling like Richard Nixon as he says that, he doesn't want to apologize to his heroes for that either; he will let that statement ride on the buoyancy of the fetid air, beer farts and bourbon swill covering his body, his pores smell from a three day cold sweat, he blows his nose on his undershirt, walking back and forth, trying to remember the guy's name in *War and Peace* who inhabited the terrain of his madness by taking it at right angles, walking his steps at ninety degree turns, he wants to say Edelstein, but realizes that's Michael's best friend's name, he's only doing that because he likes the guy and would like to get drunk with him one of these days, no one speaks to him anymore, no one.

The fucking kids, he says, the kids, respect respect respect, saying the word too often, it loses all its anger, dissipating into a poor imitation of (is that what he wants?) a woman's feeling she gets from a man, the man pulling out her chair in the restaurant, letting her sit down first, bowing, screwing, eating her out afterward, he's shaking, Leland, not sure if it's from the booze or the thoughts running through his head, the lack of booze or the lack of thoughts running through his head, trotting through his brain, walking, jauntily, through the tulips planted behind his eyes.

Respect.

That's a quality that Leland has, even if his mother was a town pump, his father was all right, he likes Inspector Coole.

Michael, Emmett, the girls hating the old man for being a bastard, Lee can't blame him, the old guy works all day on the dock and comes home to his cruddy wife who hasn't made the dinner yet, drunk on her ear playing with the kids next door, or if she's cooked the dinner, it's always burnt; god, she's a loser that woman, he says, "not just her, Sam, Oona, Deirdre, all of them," his old girlfriend Shea McKinsey, what a name, with her big tits and freckly face, he loved her, he loved her, he loved her, used to go over to her house every night after he got thrown out of the novitiate, he'd say to his friend Charlie, "I'm going to Chez Shea," whacking him on the ass; what are you talking about what are you talking about, Charlie'd say, bouncing off his punch and coming into Leland's belly with his own playful right cross; Leland living with Charlie through two marriages in Connecticut, he ruined the first one, but Charlie decided he wanted to make the second work, he asked Leland to leave, and Lee pulled out into space once more, wiggy, he toured the house his family lived in, tearing down the icons, breaking the windows, stomping through the rooms till all nerves centered there had the unhooked feeling of his own; Leland and Charlie'd sit in his MG, weighing down the shocks to the ground, because Charlie weighed the same as Leland, the both of them in the yard all night, because Charlie didn't make it back to his wife, he'd give you the psycho rundown on Leland, where he went wrong, how he should be treated (C. being a social worker), and come dawn, he'd be crying on Leland's shoulder, the two of them like hippo lovers in a sports car, Charlie was an orphan, Charlie was misunderstood by his wife, Charlie in the end wanted to be Leland.

"Let's go talk to your old man," Charlie says, bawling his filthy orphan eyes out.

They'd wake up Inspector Coole, who'd rampage through the house at dawn, "never in my life, I tell you, it's the wackiest thing I've heard of," because Charlie was in the living room, crying, he wanted to be his son, it was unnerving even for the strong.

When Lee got out of the Army, they gave him an honorable discharge, even though they declared him Section 8 inadvertently, he couldn't be bossed around by Georgia sergeants with watermelon for brains; earlier Lee went partying in Spain, AWOL, with his buddy Carson from Oregon, a big Nordic from a lumberjack family, he was nothing like his brother Emmett calling the cops to take him away or Mickey Mack Coole, the hotshit author now; Leland is thinking, Michael was blinded not to realize that all women dump you, finally, it's inherent in their species, inferior so they try to compensate for their lack of intelligence by being ruthless, women, Leland danced with them in Spain, he was a good dancer, it wasn't so much his partner, as long as he had something to twirl around, say a broom even, and drunk four days, he wound up in a church bell tower, raving, calling down his wrath upon the Spanish, the USA, its Army, the family, mostly them, for he felt that structure stunk.

It's because the mother is the center of the household, he says, "you can see what it does when you go to Ireland, just look at those vacant, hungry, sad pusses on my father's relatives," you know right off, the women rule their household, its these hags that have ruined the world.

Rubens was the only painter who portrayed that breed correctly, pink & fat.

Now if I could get my hands on one of those revolutionary Jewish girls from SDS, one of those fat girls from the Bronx with Army fatigues on, handing out pamphlets on how to stop the war in Vietnam, & not pretty, let her be dirty as the floor in this cellar I'm drunk in, no where to go, I'm back home, & it's not bad, I give the old lady twenty-five bucks a week for rent & food, buy four cases of beer a week from the distributor who delivers, five bottles of bourbon every ten days, I just sit, staring at the large S on the first page of Ulysses,

Stately

That's a word I like, for even though I'm floundering in the swill of my own fat, I still imagine those days when my chest was puffy & my waist was like a small hoop, that's no lie, I had spunk enough to run around, I'd even be laid now if I hadn't lost my memory, the will to continue, the nerve to split this house.

But a fat Jew in Army fatigues, a real bagel baby.

The trouble with my brothers, Emmett goes off & marries a tacky Italian from Ithaca, New York, she has formica dreams & plastic on the sofa, take off your shoes when you walk in the living room, that kind of thing, & Michael, the great bard, gets sucked in by letting a skinny bitch from Boston's proper support him from

43

*money her family probably conned out of Irish working
class dogs.*

*I went to a reading Michael gave at a bookstore on
the lower east side, drinking in this Polish bar on Second
Avenue, it was like the old times, the kid had a little
spunk in him still, downing Bushmills with me, we were
like Dean Moriarty & Sal Paradise,* "red brick . . . walk
up . . . alley . . . clutter. . . ," *those old words go pop
in my head like a magic cartoon, when I think how I
used to sit for hours with Michael in the attic, both of us
listening to the one poetry record we had, Jack Kerouac
reading with Steve Allen doing backup piano.*

"Charlie Parker looked like Buddha . . . Nirvana
. . . rollicking whawhoo . . . bam . . . we are all nothing . . . the flower is nothing . . . the sun is nothing
. . . women, nothing . . ."

*Like that song that Tuli Kupferberg sings with the
Fugs. Nothing is nothing, goddamn, sitting in this bar
belting down shots, & we show up to the reading late,
me cracking up with Mickey Mack Coole sitting up there
with a podium in front of him, I keep remembering how
I turned him on to books,* On the Road, Ginger Man,
Edna Saint Vincent Millay, Hemingway, *& the fuck
never would admit that he liked Hemingway, always
leaning toward that faggy French thing,* poète maudit *or
something, but he's great tonight, rapping fast, not slow
& calculated like the audience wants a poet to be, he's
running words into each other, I can tell he learnt well
from that record, all the other kids out on Long Island,
either Jewish intellectuals or Christian hub cap stealers
like his brother Emmett, always in trouble with the police, acting like a lizard because the doctors told him he's*

44

going to die in two years, but tonight, Mickey Mike like the bards from O'Coole, he snaps into his stuff & me shouting him on like Paul Gonzalez wailing a twenty-seven chorus solo sax on that Duke Ellington album in Newport, doing the interlude between "Diminuendo & Crescendo in Blue," I'm rapping my knuckles on the seat in front of me in time to the beat, which ain't iambic, it's spacy, I'm slipping that night, I feel myself cutting out of my body again, I'm no longer Leland Coole, which is when the trouble begins. I start to think I'm Jack Kerouac, Philly Joe Jones pushing Gonzalez on, Ernest Hemingway making fun of F. Scott, I identify with everyone, that's my problem, no discretion, just begin at the top & slowly sink into the abyss, the world is caving, because I'm euphoric again, & that's the red light that warns me, pretty soon I crack up pretty soon I . . .

Then Michael breaks this reverie with a series of poems about his blond bitch who tried to have him arrested, her & her new beau, this hippie entrepreneur creep who looks too hip to trust, nothing like the beats who you feel comfortable with after the first swig on a bottle of wine, he starts to read these sick poems of love, pining, it's a bad posture, you have to learn to stick your chest out, belt these rags in the mouth when they act up, "you sound like Poe with his lost Lenore, you hump," I yell to him, & the girl of my dreams, the one running the reading tonight, she turns around & tells me to shut up while Michael is reading, I was going to tell her where to get off, who I was, but I wasn't sure myself, it was either James Dean or the French playwright Arrabal, what could I tell her, this revolutionary in her khakis, & pictures of Fidel all around her store, she was the girl I had been waiting for all my life, fat & scarred & radical, but she never would have believed me.

Back to the slough.

My mind blanks, I can't remember a thing, the room frightens me, this cellar I'm in, where?

Say it over again: Longgisland, Mineola, Coole house, father's cellar, oldest son, a.k.a. "Chubby," "Beefy," "Lee," James Dean! There I go slipping, because I'm staring at the memorabilia scattered over the floor, empty beer cans, ripped ID, ripped wallet, fist through plywood wall the night before when I heard myself again, & that picture at twelve years old, when my hair was pushed back in a DA, collar up on my pink shirt, my buck teeth actually handsome looking, the heir to the throne of O'Coole, but the O vanished when they came to America, so they could get through immigration faster, alphabetically, & you thought that only happened to Zimmermans, Mr. Dylan! I'm trying to trace with my finger along the lines of my forehead, find out just where I was talking, what I was talking about?

"Hey, Leland, want to play basketball with me?"

Terry Coole, my brother, now I remember, I'm Leland, the fierce, a little group therapy in Florida after my twelfth shock, Terry is my doctor, not my fifteen year old brother, because if he was my brother, I'd break that guitar over his head, doesn't he realize that there's only going to be one Bob Dylan this century, doesn't Michael realize there was only one Jack Kerouac, I am Hemingway.

"You want to play or not?"

Getting discharged from the Army, coming home to find out when I called her up, Shea was married, she

46

hooked up with a greaseball who worked in a garage in
Suffolk County.

"I hate women, you!!"

Terry running up the stairs.

"Mom, Leland is going crazy again. All the pages of
his books are ripped up on the floor & he's writing crazy
things on the mirrors."

OTTO * PIG * GOD * I ARE THE ART
FART * HOMOGENIZE THEM

It makes perfect sense these words, mirrored on their
walls for posterity, the perfect prosody, that's all, the
world reduced to where it reflects The Word on his face,
he is watching the mole on the left side of his nose grow
like a spore in a black forest, & the old man is screaming, "I'll call the police, he's disrupting my house again.
He's too old to be living here with young kids, I'll have
him put away." Go to violence, that shuts them up.

Razor in hand.

The first Coole to move gets his throat cut, they freeze.

They are scared shitless because of his size & the terror he inspires in them. Don't he know it, from mother
to father on down the faces of the children, he could
wipe them out, all, make page 3 of the *Daily News.*

FORMER MENTAL PATIENT GOES BERSERK
KILLS ENTIRE FAMILY WITH RAZOR

But Michael & Emmett would get out of the slaugh-
ter, because they don't come by anymore, he'd hunt them
down like he did Michael once, when he knew Mackool

47

was tapping his brain for ideas in those books he wrote, that nurd, he's the one Leland wants to get, cut off his typing fingers, bleed out his tongue, inject blue ink in his veins, but wait, they're frightened to move, they don't realize that Lee's more afraid than they are, & they're thinking it a complex burden from god to house a mentally ill son, "I'm scared, damnit!" & the walls closing in like that, the words bunching in his head so that Lee forgets his name, he's lying on that table again with that cracker attendant attaching rubber plugs to his head to short out his Northern venom, why doesn't one of them love Leland understand him give the boy a hand Sam . . .

She's backing away from him, she's saying to her father:

"He's going to hit me again."

"Call the police, quick," the old man says.

Traitor, I'll hang you by your balls that look like soft shell clams out of the shell.

"His eyes are buggy," the old man screams.

"Get the police," he says again, pushing Terry toward the phone, Terry runs out the door.

"I just wanted to play basketball."

Snap.

Leland's just kidding and they go call the cops, rough him up, but this entire Island is mad, they won't keep him for more than a night, the nut wards filled with terrified men, slaves to their fantasies, Lee is back to the cellar, he keeps saying he wasn't going to hurt them, wielding the razor in his hand, he cuts himself, letting the blood flow down his pant leg, a dirty pool of rusty red mixes with the floor dirt, he's trying to see his reflection in the blood, but all he gets is a reflection from the light, dancing giddily over the surface of the brown-red blood puddle, the house is quiet again, though this time, silence comes through with an ominous buzz, the air is like air on a battleground after a seige by General Patton, the house lies ravaged, Private Leland Coole billets himself in the cellar for rest and solace, he is going over the war strategy of living in this house, he's thinking, his sadness helps to restore a balance to this house, keeps an equilibrium, that each derangement of the children acts as a check and balance system, there is no King of the Hill, Serfs, he says, we are peasants, he's farming this feudal land in the basement, trying to make life, harvest a fertile crop from this arid soil, it won't work, Lee, it can't, he says . . .

He's trying to bend over for a glass of bourbon, but the rolls of his fat around the stomach won't allow him to bend, he was talking about battle, then it became a pasture, the sun was shining in the meadow, the children romping through alfalfa, yellow yellow, all of them waspy and prosperous, the mother and father beautiful to look at, to watch move, animal like, with all grace upon them, Leland saw it all through a vaselined lens, impressionistic, blending with each other, harmonious, he saw himself thin, high cheekboned, Indian in the way he moved with ease among the harvest, barefoot, he wore a dark mustache, carrying a white straw hat in his hand, off-white suit, white bucks, there was a drink for lunch, but he drank it in deference to his comely mother and father, newly returned from the continent, the father telling him about the new art works he bought, that they would have a look at the new collection after lunch, Leland sipped a Margarita, he felt athletic, having run a mile before lunch, he played a game of squash with his brother Emmett, a prominent lawyer in New York City, chatting with his brother's wife, he took her arm, brotherly, and together they wended their way through the orchard, finding other members of the Coole family situated around the picnic table, the maid just laying out the tablecloth, Emmett's wife offered to help the girl, but Leland frowned saying, "she was hired to do that, it's her job," taking Emmett's wife by the arm again, they drifted over to the stable, Leland wanted to show her his new race horse.

Then it erupted.

The dream broke over his body in a cold sweat, he was back to his cell, the dampness clogged his nostrils, his eyes focused on, it was gray, he stammered, stuttered, flopped from the bed, the razor in his hand, he was looking for order, Lee wanted to dismiss the chaos, but they wouldn't grant him that one wish, the children screamed louder, the father got frantic, the mother was spaced out.

But he was talking, then the abyss sucked him under, back to Florida his grave.

They'll want him out of the house this evening, tomorrow morning, soon.

Lee says, there are nine others where his cancer runs short, the old lady'll get drunk, one of the kids will get suspended from school for fighting or smoking, Emmett will have a fight with his wife and need a place to sleep, always a lunatic rampant within the confines of these walls, the living room painted a Puerto Rican blue, the

whole house smelling of alcohol, dampness, failure with
the old man in his bedroom, he's bathing his ingrown toenail, he's imagining himself Joseph Kennedy, a band of
sons who will rule America; Leland is aware that his father looks at him like a John F. Kennedy who flopped
from the start, right at that moment when he fired the
first torpedo in World War II, the Kennedys he says, that
name, a bunch of Irish crooks, he tells himself, the
Cooles are better off even with flops, false starts, miscal-
culations, he says that he should care if they throw him
out tomorrow, the oldest son, the heir apparent, the future president of our country.

Mickey Mack Coole is the only one who doesn't come
back after his defeats, Leland thinks that the third son
makes the rest of the family think that Mackool doesn't
have losses, but by the fact his last name is Coole Michael is damned from the git go, a tribe of fuckups that's
what we are, he says, hopeless, uneducated, opinionated,
clumsy, the old man won't let Mickey Mike in the house,
because he says his son is a dirty writer, and the few
times they've met, silence, they hate each other worse
than lovers; Leland can see the other one spitting on the
grave of whoever dies first, like what Dominic Behan
said about his brother Brendan at the cemetery:

"It's the first time I've been in his company when he
didn't monopolize the conversation."

Bernadette Devlin, you're next! Lee screams up the
stairs.

Where did he go again?

Michael had enough smarts though, Lee says, you
can't take that away from him, running away from home
when he was fifteen years old and never showing up

again until that night when he quit college, the family didn't even know that he had been in college, and Leland crazy that night too, he wanted to sympathize with the bard, but his head shaved on one side, his clothes ripped in the sartorial manner of the unhinged, Lee broke four doors that night, broke three windows in the kitchen, smashed a chair in the living room, he had them hopping, loving every minute of his performance, he awarded himself an Oscar for the best supporting actor that evening, he got his way, it was his dominion once more, he had found domain.

But fuck Michael, he decides, he can talk for himself, Lee's just getting these words floating through the cellar, he wants to leave a spell behind in case the cops come to take him away, Leland feels alchemy in his madness, that he's eaten one too many tanna leaves, the curse will wear off if he looks into a mirror or one of the children hold a crucifix in front of his face; he's back to the mirror, though he can't see his image anymore, the surface of the mirror covered with a pellicle of magic marker from his writing, phlegm, smears, sputum, there is a crack running down the middle of it, he says, "I Leland, me the terrible, will speak, you motherfuckers . . ."

High school was best for Leland, no one changes after that, they get their image tighter, know how to work their tricks better, euchre is everything, he says, for people are basically finished developing in high school— "Particularly women," he says, talking to himself in the smeared mirror, there were girls who were the prettiest cheerleaders then, the most popular snatch around, and now, breasts sagging, varicose veins, stretch marks, belly drawn out from babies, scars from Caesarians—he, Leland thought of himself, at least had an excuse. Back then he was the King of Groove, dead center with his sweat shirt sleeves cut at the shoulders, the hippest symbol to emerge from the fifties since people wore the collars of their shirts up, playing bongos, drinking beer at Jones Beach, now you can only buy it at the refreshment stand, two at a time, but back then, drunker than the kingfish, he'd guzzle cases in the dunes and run into the surf delirious from the sun, his crowd thought Lee crazy, but crazy in the groovy sense, he was slick, because the second thing Leland had, besides his good teeth, and he was the only member in the Coole family who did have good teeth, Lee was a great swimmer, body surfing, you name it, he'd crash into the white foamy center of a breaking wave, let the undertow swirl his body around like seaweed, fan-fucking-tastic!

But the things you love, he mumbled, tearing pages out of his best books, the Hemingway, the Kerouac, throwing the pages in a pile on the floor, the things you love are the things that bring you closest to death, he said. Shit, drunker than a pig, you wouldn't catch him talking like that unless he was already gone in his head, but said, he was not one to retreat, having said too many things to retract from his life, onward, he yelled, this time he had a British accent, though he thought it sounded Irish, he felt like Errol Flynn, one leg perched on his mattress, the other bare foot standing in the coagulated pool of his blood; the hand had stopped bleeding and he removed the underpants he wrapped around the cut, onward, you literate bastards into his skull, he's going to upset this house today, have them laughing, that's his weapon. To tell the funniest jokes while dying, slowly, day to day, because his soul was gone, he knew he had had one because he felt the absence of that organ this moment, a hollow nauseous feeling quaking in his stomach, the emptiness drilled through his head, he wanted his audience to hold on to his corkscrew tail, he was a sinking piggy, though a swimmer, he kept repeating in his bored out, hollowed out brain, thoughts echoing now from the bareness of his mind, the inside of his brain smooth and glowing like a bowling ball, Lee stuck his fingers down his throat to force himself to puke, but nothing came up, a little spit a little blood, he hadn't eaten in two days, bourbon bourbon . . .

The world's oldest three hundred pound virgin will go manly, he thought.

Mensch.

Machismo.

¡El hombre borracho, como no!

BLAM!

Leland wasn't a marskman, sharpshooter, expert, he didn't like guns, but a swimmer, he was that, yes, he could swim to death, it was the proper way to die, by the sea by the sea, cabanas open with flappers coming out, they are singing that song. *"By the beautiful sea,"* like kewpie dolls, bald cunts and painted eyes from a factory, Leland listened to the song, as he thought about the ocean, he was bugged that his thoughts weren't grave at such an austere moment in his life, but radio, television, newspapers, he was heir to bad tastes on the planet, and that song was the only refrain he knew then, he was hoping for a quote he could remember from Keats, just a phrase, but it wouldn't come through, then he was thinking of his Uncle Bill, mother Rose's brother, she says he was thrown overboard, off a tanker near the East Coast of Africa, but Leland doesn't believe that, he says, he jumped overboard, the world knows that pursers are faggots, he probably couldn't live with the thought of all those mad ladies in the household, splash, Leland sees his uncle taking the plunge, swallowing the salt water, bobbing a few times, then sinking down with his lungs filled up with water, splash, an instant later, he'd be drowning, forcing himself to drown, since he was too good a swimmer otherwise.

That morning he remembered the story about Evelyn Waugh trying to commit suicide by drowning, not sure whether he made it up or heard the tale, Leland, as he said, faked his reading habits, but he often got to know a writer so well in his fantasy, it was like he had read the *obras completas*. But Evelyn Waugh, he supposedly wrote this elaborate suicide note, left it on the beach and was about to do himself in, but a hundred yards out, he gets stung by a giant jelly fish, and swims back to shore, rips up the note and goes home.

Leland didn't bother with notes, there were plenty of his notebooks, misspellings, runons, the works. He couldn't be coherent with his words, the world had to catch up to him, not the reverse, they had to understand him, blagh! he said, what's it matter?

Into the waves, froth, he's like a steamer, the best whaler, chomping through the waves like a pigboat torpedo, the great Leland pigfish, a glorious swine going out for the last time, but going out, nonetheless, with as much glory as he came into the world, so long mother, you town pump, no one's going to miss him now, he'll swim till he's exhausted, maybe a few miles out, Leland will be a speck, his rotund shape reduced to a gnat on the horizon, as a few tourists with binoculars will think they spotted a whale, his arms snap through the water, the legs flailing desperately for the sacred place where he'll sink into the ocean, but fifteen minutes later, he hates the world, that is the testament he wishes to leave behind, he hates this world, can't stand himself, useless useless, all his ennui, he stops, his arms go limp the feet sink down, he's swallowing water, big gulps of green water going down his throat into his lungs, he's sinking, fighting for air, he's at the surface again, breathing like a Labrador retriever, he plunges under again, the world spinning his balance gone not sure which way is up, but to the surface once for air, he tries again, but surfaces after fifteen seconds, Leland thinks of himself as balsa, waterlogged but unsinkable, he can't do it, he loves himself, no, he hates this body, but but

Floating, he stayed out there, waterlogged, for two hours, swam back to shore and walked into the refreshment stand for two beers, cursing, he kicked sand in the faces of the old ladies, children, young girls, any creature that looked more helpless than himself, for Leland hated the weak, and he was the weakest one there in his elephant trunks.

Like the Lone Ranger, riding out of town on his steed.

"Who was that fat man?"

He walked home along the highway, twenty miles, people stopping to offer him a lift, fucking Christians, they're the worst, for by the fact they're offering, they know your desperation and want a piece of the helpless, then later they can say, "there was a pilgrim worse than us," like people who work with junkies, social workers, probation officers, those kind he thought, it was because he was fatter, more miserable, weaker. That's why Leland hated New York City, there was always a bum lower in the gutter, muddier, drunker, more down and out, no one lets you be the ideal of depravity, there's another asshole who wants to outdo you, Leland is thinking this, as he walks back from the mattress, tearing more paperback books, he begins to shred the hardcover books, starting with best sellers, working his way through the classics, he's wiping away the scum from the mirror, searching for his face, he can't find it, god the noises they're making upstairs, he's going to belt one of those kids, strangle him.

Now Michael is in jail, he thinks, he doesn't like any of this, he keeps thinking that Mickey Mack Coole did it to write a book, to impress a girl, get a job in the welfare department.

The bourbon bottle is opened.

The Protestants know how to celebrate it better, he says, and the Jews, they're the best, put a Chanukah candle in the window and drink a bottle of Manischewitz wine; these Christians, Leland says, pacing the cellar floor, his nose is filled with the smell of mildew, decay, he says, the Christians keep forgetting their leader was a Jew, but then, he says, pouring the bourbon, a calm settles him, his demons evaporate, it happens like that, he thinks, I'm in control again, that's all any of us want, to be able to manipulate our shitty lives, he says, drinking from the bottle now, they're all martyrs, let Mickey Mike rot in jail, he's got his own ass to worry about this season.

CHAPTER THREE

Oona in her room listens to "Let It Be" by the Beatles; she smokes a joint; she is so small that she knows her father, Inspector Coole, will not lay a hand to her. The other night when he hit her, Oona laid down her own law, finally. She hardly speaks, but when she does, people listen, they turn their heads, Michael or Pat have taken her to loft parties in Manhattan, crazy parties, with guests sardined between the smell of pot, alcohol and the sweat of artistic self esteem, places where power counts, size is everything, they step on creatures too small or too fragile to take their styles, small things get stomped, if they can't survive the fun, but with Oona, a tiny island of space emerged around her, this creature under five feet tall, her lovely stoned out eyes looking seductive, it was the incongruity that threw them, that she was sensual, though Oona looked about twelve years old, she had the grace of a thirty year old woman, and her face, beautiful and clear, with those penetrating eyes, that were all sex, coupled with those silences, words evaporated around her, she had destroyed a New York ideal of the free woman being this tall, stately child that slinked from martini to reefer like a show dog, Oona floated, and where she went angel like, the party eyes followed her.

But Inspector Coole ruined his scene that night last week, when he hit Oona, after he threw out her boyfriend, a long haired teen-age pusher, whom the old man tried to run over with his car, honestly, that same night, and Oona, the blood rising, she was so compact that the pressure from her anger was greater than say Leland's, if he got angry, she had her temper that each Coole has seen break loose about three times in her life, the third being last week with the old man, he slapped her hard across the face, a gesture he performed too liberally with the children, his own and others in his house, even a daddy has to pay dues.

She stood there boiling up, her face contracting, she spit out her words:

"Fuck you!"

That was all, it was plenty.

Unlike her tantrums as a child—they were wicked —her young woman concision—Dichtung—sliced through, it was the only words she had said to him probably in five years, her daddy knew she meant it, he was crying later.

But her venom had its effect.

59

The old man would not bug her anymore, and even tonight, the house in Bedlam, there was a three foot aureole around Oona, which the old man knew he couldn't venture into, her tripping and smoking grass in her room at sixteen, he wasn't going to raise an objection, he was overridden, since she had founded her own province that even a Hun couldn't pillage.

She was in her room during the commotion, not believing a word about Michael being in Bellevue, she had visited him five nights ago, telling him of her bout with the old man, they got stoned together, he showed her new writing, and they went out to dinner at an Italian restaurant around Bleecker Street with one of his girlfriends, Michael was looking good, he was together, Oona knew there was a mistake.

Oona was part of an immutable triumvirate, since she and Patrick painted, that consisted of Michael, Patrick and herself, three of the Coole tribe she thought would survive the malaise, because they had their art, which wasn't necessarily in their actual work, but more in the spiritual rhythms they had set up in their lives, she was smoking a joint, talking to Deirdre, her younger sister, who Oona thought was too young to begin getting high, but who knew about the process at twelve years old.

They were talking girl talk, Deirdre got her first period the day before.

"Mother Rose said we should eat a fudge sundae three times in our lives," Oona said to Deirdre, one of the plump ones in the Coole family.

"Once when you get your period. When you lose your virginity. And once when you get pregnant."

She told Deirdre that they'd both have fudge sundaes tomorrow.

Deirdre, a little slow, asked why Oona intended to have one too.

"This is going to be my second one, Deirdre," she said, rolling another joint, she slipped it into her pocket for just before she went into Midnight Mass a few hours away.

CHAPTER FOUR

"The Beast" tooled his red Volkswagen, the engine hummed with its fine tuning, All Hail and Beware! Hallelujah, The Beast, alias Emmett Coole, who'd take off his pants, not to screw, but to show off his dickie, at the slightest mention of, "let's drop trow at the party tonight," he was the inventor of the Moon, that is, he first started the fad, where in a car you pull alongside another car, your car preferably a station wagon, and from each window starboard side, facing the other car's port, the occupants in the wagon, dropped their pants and stuck their furry asses, bared, out the window to the consternation, amazement or pleasure of the other car. Scrawny, but big peckered, Emmett early acquired his name for this feat; an escape from his death bed in a hospital, where he disguised himself as a nun; pissing from the top of the water tower, way up in the firmament, on his high school English teacher's head; there were many virtuoso accomplishments by the lad, and his old tag was not unfounded for this reason. Emmett tooled his red Volkswagen off the Long Island Expressway at the proper exit to his home, the light turning amber, he downshifted the car, almost hitting, a side swipe to the car waiting at the light, shifted again and had the bug up to sixty-five in seconds.

"A super charged engine," he said, proud with the speed of his deceptive machine.

The little lady, his new wife, had thrown him out for Christmas, because he got drunk after an AA (Alcoholics Always) meeting, lost his job, didn't go to his night class at the Community College, he was hanging with his old buddy JT "Lucky" MacDuffy, a notorious asshole from Long Island, who had moved to Manhattan recently, but without changing or sophisticating this fellow, Lucky remained in tact as stupid as he had begun on the planet, half witted, violent, pathological, self assured of his greatness. He in fact sat next to The Beast in the killer seat of the VW, or rather kneeling, since his fly was open and he was pissing out the window, the urine mist shooting mostly toward the back seat. They were drunk; they were happy, no, they were simply drunk, thoughtless, and content with their familiarity and vulgar ways, if not brothers, then joined in arson and petty theft as though by sodder.

This boy Emmett, a blond haired brother, was sandwiched between Michael and Leland, and spent most his delinquent time with JT, stinko in alleys or jugged in the drunk tank can, the criminal brace were averaging each a half quart can of beer every two miles, or as JT put it, the mathematician, "a beer a minute, Beast," and feeling contumacious and nostalgic, brother Emmett said:

"Got that old trouble feeling soaking me, JT," his eyes half lidded from a bender, bloodshot, he swerved the car, pulled out of the fishtail on the snowy road, straightened out, and kept the machine farting along at sixty, through red lights, and JT going, "crack my sides, Beast, you are a pisser."

This was true.

His kidneys were in terrible shape, as well as his stomach, his lungs, his pimply face, his rectum, his eyes from hayfever, his nose from unfixed breaks, his skinny bones, which he had but one set of, were fractured and broken from infinite brawls, scuffles, misunderstandings, fights.

"What's the trouble?"

The Beast expounded.

"It's not as bad as my brother Leland, I got an excuse for the way I act. My fuckups are accountable for."

"What's that, Beast?" JT asked, pronouncing his name with great warmth and feeling.

"My sickness, when I was a kid. I almost died when I was fourteen years old from colitis. Down to seventy-five pounds, the doctors said I was going to die at sixteen years old. What did you expect me to do, become a saint."

"No," Lucky said, thinking of how they snuck him out of Mercy Hospital disguised as a nun. "You had every right to live the way you did with that over your head."

"So I became a drunk," he said, not hearing Lucky.

JT nodded his head as though the story were a new one for him.

"My trouble is, I'm alive at twenty-seven and I'm acting still like I'm fifteen about to die in one year."

"You took the words out of my mouth," Lucky said, still trying to piss out the window, and not clear enough in his intentions to ask his friend to pull over to the side of the road.

"Seriously, that's what happened."

"You got an excuse for how you act," Lucky said, anticipating his friend's coda.

"Around my age, most guys first start to become juicers, but I've been one for fourteen years already."

"You got an excuse. There's no excuse for how your brother Leland acts."

Emmett cut him short.

"Watch what you say about Lee, he's my brother."

"OK, OK! You're the one who brought it up."

"He got burned in Florida," Emmett said, feeling queasy in his beer for defending that which he hated. But he reasoned that it was all right within the family to put each other down, but without, the world should fuck off with their sociology.

Emmett here should be explained from Go, that moment he crashed out from mother Rose's womb smack into the hands of his older brother Leland.

There are three incidents that shroud this filial animosity, with addendums to this list coming in by the day.

The first for Emmett occurred at five years old, everyone then simply called him Emmett; he was pudgy, blond, cute, a handsome American baby.

Leland stuck Emmett's hand in the hot oven, that was when they lived in Brooklyn, around the corner from Grandma Coole, Emmett still shows the scars, whenever a member of Coole is trying to figure how Leland went off his head this time, E. says:

"He was a sadist even then."

Showing them his scarred hand.

The second was when Leland pushed Emmett off a billboard, advertising the first 3-D movie in the neighborhood, *Fort Ticonderoga*.

The last happened within the last five years, when Emmett was hiding from the police for one his crimes; he was sitting at three in the morning in the local diner, figuring he was safe there, since it was the most likely place he would be, and Leland walked in after a poker game at the caddy shack at the golf course; Emmett told him what he was doing, and Leland, without wincing or, later he was to say, without malice, went to the phone booth, called the police, and told them where they might be able to find their culprit, his brother Emmett, The Beast.

"I've done something for your own good," Leland said to his brother, "and you might not understand it now, but later I'm sure you'll realize I did this because I love you."

"What did you do this time, you fuck!"

"Sit down and let me treat you to breakfast."

Like the condemned man's last meal, was what was on Lee's mind, and Emmett didn't trust his gracious offer. He got up to leave, and saw the police bubbles going outside, so into the bathroom he went, out the window, they caught him, handcuffed him, booked him at the station house, he slipped out another window, they caught him again, and he slipped out the next room they placed him in. This exit, escape, seizure, and re-exit continued for some months, and then he was convicted, paroled, and back to his old habits again, the ones he'd grown to love from re-use and tested fidelity to his intentions, and each time, his lawyer got him off by pleading to the judge about a particular physical defect in the boy that called for sympathy and not confinement.

"He has only a year to live, your honor."

Clemency was administered, since they felt they would be rid of the blond thin menace within the year, and a pleasant following year it would be, the officials thought, with the Beast dead and buried, his younger brothers and sisters incapable of surpassing his depravity; it was a blessing that the Emmetts in the world died young and unloved, they thought, for there would be no end foreseeable had his body been constructed so as to endure the abuse he inflicted upon it. But instead his name grew larger, his notoriety in hoodlum circles reached fantastic and exaggerated heights, because he once beat up a cop and this act endeared him forever with the cream of delinquency. Then there was a fight in another bar, the now 110-pound animal Coole, Emmett, throwing the bartender down the shuffle board machine, and scoring a strike, he scored a knockout, a dragged out evening, where Lucky, ever alongside the Beast, knew the arresting officer, who let them go, because "we used to rob appliance stores together," the cop said to Emmett, pointing his night stick toward Lucky, beaming. This fortunate occurrence coupled the creative energies of the three into a small underworld of crime that pivoted around a warehouse in Brooklyn, where Lucky and Emmett drove several times a week, picked up two suitcases, and delivered them to a destination on Long Island.

They were given guns, but Emmett pawned his for drinks one afternoon and Lucky seldom loaded his, though he liked to flash it late at night, while drunk, in one of his many haunts on the main drag. They were paid seventy-five dollars each every time they made a delivery, and the cop taught them new ways to circumvent the law, and each morning, with his newly moneyed world, his body taxed enormously from these criminal excursions, he bought new implements for his physical ailments.

First off, The Beast was fastidious, you couldn't touch his clothes. He had his own room, personal laundry and cleaning service, a maid to come in once a week to clean his room, while the rest of the Coole mansion laid in ruin and covered with a decade's soot. Soot was Emmett's undoing, what with asthma, hayfever, and allergies up the pipe. Other undoings were foodstuffs, he had to have his own menu worked out a week in advance and given to mother Rose, who loyally catered to these needs. Wheat germs, Vitamins A through E, tincture of this and that, special eggs from special chickens in New Jersey, a bread from a bakery many towns away, Emmett would enter on a bummer into the dining room for his breakfast around noon, for he seldom attended classes in high school, because he was usually too sick to attend, though by evening his maladies often left him. He was given a tutor, but his tutor was always drunk, and when he showed up to give Emmett lessons, they usually drove off to the closest bar to confer about Thomas Hardy, Ovid, mathematics, science, or none of the above. Emmett came to breakfast in his silk bathrobe, a muffler around his neck, his fur lined slippers, a hot water bottle tucked around his waist, with thoughts of a good emetic up his ass. If any of his brothers were at home, his first thing was to check them out, sartorially, to see whether they were wearing his shoes, socks, never his pants because no one was that skinny, but Mickey Mack did fit into his shirts and sweaters. "Take off my fucking shoes, Michael, and get that sweater off your mangy back!" he'd scream, upsetting the noisy tenor of the breakfast table. "Who's been using my hair brush, that's all I want to know," he'd say, and as his mother served him his special two minute eggs poached, with the semi-warm bread with the serrated edges, the strained baby food, and his special healthy herbal tea from Great Britain, Emmett threatened new violence upon fat Mickey Mack Coole, if he did not fuck off with wearing his older brother's clothes. "You slimey, fat bastard, you stretch everything you wear," he said, calming down for his meal, popping his pills, and using his atomizer. Next came the asthmatic inhalators, respirators, injectors, resuscitators, little machines he'd insert into his nose, then pump, large machines he plugged in and breathed through, and whose voltage often shorted out, but always dimmed, the lights. Amo nitrate, ups, stomach tranquilizers, he was a working class Proust and the adolescent answer to Huysmans, and Leland complained, "With all his ailments you'd expect at least one good novel from him," he said to the bard, the brother Mackool, "and the illiterate fuck doesn't even know how to spell his name. What good is all this bullshit anyway." There were seven pills to start the day, and different alternating pills on particular hours throughout, Emmett was meticulous about this part of his life. He had a watch with an alarm, and

69

drunk, he could be unconscious with his head on the bar, the alarm rings, and he'd wake, asking the bartender for water, down his pill, and fall back to sleep on the bar. The Beast was an impeccable dresser with charge accounts at Abercrombie and Fitch, Brooks Brothers, elegant hair dressers, manicurists, at steam rooms, health clubs, small and expensive men's shops, none of which he ever paid.

"Sick or not," Inspector Coole said to his wife, "I'm tired of these threatening letters from bill collectors."

"But he's dying."

The Inspector was furious.

"He can die then without putting me in the poor house, can't he?"

"He's sick," mother Rose said.

"Then why's he want these clothes for, if he's going to die soon. I tell you, that bum's a phony if I ever saw one. He doesn't know what sick means."

"I was a nurse," mother Rose said, becoming indignant, "and when I say sick, I know what I'm talking about."

"He'll outlive us all," the father said, but mother Rose wouldn't hear of this nonsense and went out to the kitchen to prepare Emmett his herbal tea before he arrived home.

The Coole family were not on Emmett's mind now, as he drove the VW toward home, nor were they seldom there except when he had troubles, which were frequent to him, and then he would find blame. "The good thing about a large family," he said to JT, "is that I can always find me a scapegoat when I feel screwed up." There was something damaged in The Beast, he knew this himself, but he had run out of people to blame this evening, and instead he searched for old faithful memories he might share with Lucky. First, there was his father, not as a good memory but as one to blame, who beat him, once broke a stickball bat over his head, never sympathized with his ills, treated him badly, poorly, cruelly, he thought. He said to JT: "The only time my father likes me is when I get arrested. He'll bail me out, take me drinking, showing me off to his bar friends—the terror of Long Island—and by evening, when we're in front of my mother, he's downing me, berating me, calling me a downright fuckup and blot on his name." JT nodded ubiquitously, zipping his fly and licking piss off his fingers. Then Emmett, he could blame his mother, who The Beast thought catered more toward Leland and Michael, no matter how much she waited on him, how long she listened to his grief, at the end she was a bitchy old mother to him. Then there was his intestines, what was left of them, what awful pains! but incapable of stopping the flow of drink, the pang grew fiercer until it disordered his brain into a miserable pea of hate for his brothers and sisters. Michael was a sissy too, and no matter how smart he got, Emmett thought, and no matter how skinny I get, I can still beat the shit out of him every time. "I never liked your brother Michael," JT said. "He always acts like those smart Jews in school, too smart for their own good." Emmett was going to tell him to fuck off with criticism of his brother, but having defended one already tonight, it was too much to go defending another he probably disliked as much as he dis-

71

liked Leland. "He's a penis all right," Emmett said. But he thought it was good to have Mackool near, for when Emmett was bored, there was always his younger brother's flabby belly to punch and torture until JT came over with news of a party or bar to go to. The only thing left for Emmett was his sentimental memories of crime with JT, for he couldn't think of any good things about his family.

Interesting, interesting, interesting, fabulous and unheard of nights these were, and mish-mashed through his brain, they scrambled, bitty fragments popping through his skull like hair, and shared a million drunken nights with JT, these memories, shaved from the bark of experience, and whittled, they were dredged up as the reserve conversation for those times that Lucky and Emmett got drunk enough past violence to be nostalgic for their wicked ways, and mulled over, dog-eared memories that Emmett vowed to his brother Mickey Mack Coole, he would one day surpass him by writing about these things, they blew through his mind like wind, and winded up on his tongue muddled, a blend of lie, self deception, truth, and morbid free form alcohol hysteria, Emmett pulled the car to the side of the road, and before going home, he and JT sat idling over these things like two movie fans talking plots of their favorite late night horrors, it was touching, moving, and cause to wet one's pants, which both Lucky and Emmett did at alternate times that night in their drunkenness.

"You remember the pink Ford convertible," The Beast started.

"I sure do," Lucky said, glassy eyed nostalgia.

72

"One hundred bucks it cost us, and those fake plates and phony registration and insurance, man, wow!"

"Then when your father stole the keys one night from you, and drove it into the sandpit, boy!"

"I'll never forget how when we first had it and that cop stopped us for registration check, and you snuck around behind him and hit him over the head with the blackjack, crazy, huh?"

They were laughing and wacking each other on the back.

Beer was dribbling down their chins, and often when they thought hard enough how funny the past was, they'd choke on their beer and simultaneously spit mouthfuls over each other.

"Then you put that daisy or something in his hand and we left him on the side of the road, oh boy, I'll never forget that!"

"Me either, I'll never forget that!"

"What a pisser!"

"A fucking pisser," JT or Emmett said.

Emmett went on to tell how the next morning the police came to the Coole mansion looking for him, and Michael answered the door in his underwear, they grabbed him, one of them punching him in the stomach, he fell on the floor, almost puking, he was stunned, shaking, Michael never could take it, Emmett said, being a coward when it came to investigative methods like these, another kicked him in the side, mother Rose trying to fight them off, and one punching her away too. The cop who was bopped the night before played it up with a huge bandage on his head, like he'd just come back from Iwo

Jima that moment, he said benignly, "he's not the one, it's his brother . . ."

"It don't matter, it's the same blood," a real honest dyed in blue porker, piggish in the face that only certain Eastern dicks can be, astoundingly dumb and pinkishly fat, he said, grinning as he spoke, and denying that he hit mother Rose when she ran up to them, as another cop, more familiar with the family of Coole, said:

"We'd need the entire force to beat in the heads of this family, they've got an army of about twenty."

With literal Rosey:

"There's eleven now, since Aidan died a few years ago."

He sneered and stared at her, contemptuously.

"Shut up, you, and get your son here quick!"

"You can't tell me what to do, this is my house. Where are your papers to come in here?"

He reached over to one of the many newspaper piles and handed her a copy of the *Daily News,* dated six years earlier to the day, the headline:

COP SLAYER FOUND IN HOBOKEN

Rosey was red, boiling.

"I say get out, now get out!!!"

She let out a scream that carried for blocks.

The Inspector was downstairs with his badges, his Knights of Columbus card, an epaulet from his U.S. government uniform; Leland was there with his underpants falling off, the children—how they were wonderful in these cases!—gathered around the police like a slew of Oliver Twists, poor and depraved looking like a Dickens

74

dream of squalor, they were breaking hearts with their sobs and cries, Don't take our brother, we love him! He's only got six months to live!

"Maybe we can get a warrant to declare this house a health hazard, and then lock up the family," the blue pig death menace said, as Inspector Coole looked at his wife and said, though not to her, nor to the gathered police contingency:

"The whole kit and caboodle."

Emmett was having his morning asthma attack on the porch, as the police marched in to arrest him. Leland was calling from the other room.

"Remember the Post Office, Easter, 1916, and who you were named after!"

Mother Rose turned to Leland.

"He was named after my brother Emmett."

Leland was annoyed.

"He was not!"

Inspector Coole was once again, blown-minded, stunned, looking to his wife and older son, the gathered children, the police surrounding Emmett.

"He was named after Robert Emmett," Leland said.

But mother Rose insisted, he was named after her brother.

Terry stared at the police, who were trying to shoo the children from the room. Emmett's skinny body was draped over one cop's arms, like a cloth, and the piggish-beat-up cop with the bandage had to be restrained by two other officers.

"He's putting me on, let me kill the bastard!"

Mother Rose was in the room now.

"He looks like John F. Kennedy this minute."

The police halted, amazed.

They couldn't believe what they heard and went ahead with their arrest, as though she had said nothing.

"Long live Leopold and Loeb!" Leland shouted, as his father attempted to get him to go into the cellar.

"Emmett promised to play ball today with Patrick and me," Terry said. The baby Wolfe, but a small child then, let out a fierce yell from his playpen in the living room. They weren't giving him any attention.

The Beast was canary yellow, underlined with blue lines streaking his face, there was no air going into or coming out of his body.

"If he dies this minute, it couldn't be sooner," the Inspector said, "the way he treats his mother and father."

The children, off to the side, cried and wailed like a Greek chorus of banshee. The Inspector, their father, went about slapping bottoms and faces to silence them, but only added to the cacophony, an Ivesian symphony of dissonance and American transcendental yatter.

"The Beast is going to die on us," one cop yelled to the frantic injured cop.

But mother Rose saved things with, "He needs his blue pill, the inhalator, and his respirator, if you expect a confession from him now."

"I just step in shit," Emmett said to JT in the parked VW.

"If I hadn't beaten up that cop, I would never have gotten into that rehabilitation program the county was running for delinquents. By being on parole, and also the smartest convict in the county, I was able to go to college for awhile and to get that job at the World's Fair."

"But you wound up getting arrested then too. Remember when we stomped that shitass southern vender for trying to put the make on that stewardess you were going out with."

"There are so many good memories, JT, it makes me so sad to think about them," he said, flopping an arm around his buddy.

"We just step in shit," JT said, "we're so lucky, sometimes I think there must be a god."

Emmett stared over to his friend with tears in his eyes.

"Sometimes I feel the same way, Lucky."

They stared dumbly at the knobs on the dashboard; they fixed their eyes and things went blurry; they reeked of beer and piss, shit and corruption, and both decided they would try to go to Midnight Mass this evening.

The Beast stared at the windshield button.

"Sometimes I think He's with us, man," The Beast said, dozing and waking, itching and opening another beer.

CHAPTER FIVE

The men break windows, scream about asylums, call about fights with their wives (Wife), get arrested on grand larcenies; Terence fights with Wolfe, and Oona mooning in her room, Sam knows she's smoking weed (for after her diddy bop era, Sandra turned into, got turned around, she was hip now), Mackool saying: One day they are dumb cunts who can only say, "hoy, it's a fy-on day," in that whining Brooklyn-Long Island drawl, then they are heavies, been into the dope, traveled across the country hitchhiking, but everytime Sam asks her, she says to Oona, "I'll give you grass if you want to try it, it's not as bad as cigarettes," with the Oona smile Mona Lisa impy look she's had since a babe, then she walks out the head room, that's Sam's room, only place in the house, well, you know this already. Hookahs, stereo, pillows, Persian rugs, poofs, samovar, pasha luxury, a veritable young Jewish princess, Oona walks out of the head room, and Sam don't know what she's thinking, like Mickey Mack Coole don't know what Sam thinks, he can't get into a woman's head, his sisters' especially, they fake him out, he don't know whether he be coming or going to know what they think, or do they think, he asks? Yes, for their lives are a form of thinking how to avoid their father. Goddamn muliebrity, he says.

That's not it either, for a man looks at his sister, how? The question.

How does he look at them?

Take her name Sandra. A perfectly nice name that she likes, by the time she's two years old, there are four men already in the House of Coole, and one of these hairy persons, bigger than her too, it was Leland, yes, who decides to call her Sam to make her one of the boys. Up till she's twelve, they have her get short haircuts, butch, poor Sandra, the beautician, the maid, the department store clerk, she was the princess that her daddy dreamed of, looking like Shirley Temple when she was small, those dimples she still has, or like Leland says, "they're just birth defects." That was said on her birthday, it was Bastille Day, no, it was July 4th, no, it was, forgive this lapse from your brother, Oona, no, Deirdre, yes, now he knows, it was Sandra Sam he wanted to mention, Happy Birthday To You. Explosions, dynamite! Mother Rose had her first girl to grow up on her fourteenth birthday to have her oldest brother tell her her dimples were "holes in your cheeks," he said, lighting a firecracker, he threw it at her, catch!

"Even my cleft chin," Leland said, implying Sandra's too, because they were the members in the family with strong chins; Mickey Mack Coole and Oona with those weak chins, no chins, so that they came to be known as Pigeon and Weasel, respectively, for their vanishing chins, chinless, he goofed on them constantly, "how about a few chin ups, old boy," he'd say, grabbing the stubble on Michael's, grew a beard to become a man with a chin above his shoulder, Oona having to depend on her eyes to offset the absence, though her older sister Sam Coole, Miss Sandra, the princess of Coole, she had a jutting chin, not as large as Leland's foundation, there was that dimple in her chin, on her knees too, though this is what the good brother Leland told her:

"Even that cleft chin," taking her chin in his hand, like Hamlet holding a peach, studying it dramatically, he said, "that's a birth defect, an improper split when the genes separate, what do they call it, mitosis, something or other . . ."

Sandra endured her birth defect.

The father's dream turned out to chew gum, smoke cigarettes, cut classes in school, fail half her grades, Sandra didn't like to work on her homework, she'd rather take rides in convertibles with older guys she hung around with, how could she do it to her father, her boyfriends were Italian, gas station gangs, she hung with the heavies, ex-gang leaders from Brooklyn, rough girls who rode motorcycles, she quit high school to become a beautician, and her father, she'd have to sneak out of the house to go on dates, he didn't like her doing that, the irony being, he thought her vagrant, desolate, a bad girl, and though she palled with hoodlums, she didn't lose her cherry till, when did she, sir?

Mackool wrote in his notebook that Oona found in the attic:

"Sandra stopped by occasionally, but I still don't know her the way I know Oona, say, though with all my sisters I have those fantasies, the intimate coupling after a night of marijuana and wine, undressing the oldest sister, getting down in the dirt of this apartment to explode upon each other, it was not weird like I thought it was when I was young, grab Sandra feel her up and down, post office, kissy. Though Sandra, sister Sam, I don't know, nor do I presume to know, you; it comes difficult to speak of you, because, well, you were next to me in a lot of the encounters with the old man, we were the closest in age, though emotionally I was hooked with Leland and Emmett, and not going out with girls till I was about nineteen years old, what proper perception can I bring to talk about you, I know the surfaces, but why oh why, Sam Coole, do you do the things you do?"

Her first boyfriend was a liar and a cheat.

He had done seven years for armed robbery, was in his late twenties, though he told the father he was but seventeen, he moved like a young Jorge with tattoos covering his body, snakes in combat with the wiry veins of his dark right arm, devils smiling cartoon like from his left bicep, a nude girl on his left forearm that spread her legs when he tensed his muscles, two birds above the nipples, a skull tattooed on his right ankle, pierced ear, no teeth, which still has nothing to do with Sam Coole, except that she hung with this walking art gallery in her younger days, he stole cars for her, presenting them like jewels on the front stoop to his girl Sandra, she blushed with admiration at his bravery, as he danced away from her father coming at him with the handle of a mop, "I told you not to come around here anymore, Stiletto," he yelled, chasing him around the shrubbery, Johnny Stiletto, the men in the house called him, grabbed his girl Sam, had his car engine idling in expectation of this encounter, escorted her to her seat, peeling out in the old man's face.

"My own daughter," he kept saying, walking back to the house minus a girl minus her boyfriend he intended to bag for the collection he hung over his bed like stuffed deer heads, "my oldest daughter," he said to Terry, who was playing catch with Wolfe, they couldn't understand his grief.

This is what the boys see of Sam Coole.

She is furtive, sneaking out of the house, while all are sleeping, the old man wakes up, chases her down the block, this is the way he shows his affection for his Shirley Temple.

"But even Shirley Temple sold out," Emmett said to cheer up his father.

"Wacky . . . wacky . . . wacky," Inspector Coole said, mumbling the observation into his stein of warm beer on the dining room table.

A beautician, maid, department store clerk.

Sandra was short, dark, she looked Italian, though flat chested, she didn't have the bazooms of her mother, a nice ass, heavy legs that swelled up when she worked on her feet in a beauty parlor, what the hell can an older brother say about his sister, what can he do?

Leland was sitting in Sam's room as she passed him the hookah, the tanks moving down the block, the town lay in rubble, they were the last ones left, he touched her hand, she came to him, lying on the bed next to him, a candle burnt a low flame, the electricity went when they blew up the power plant, he fondled her, running his fingers through the nappy hair that all the children in Coole grew, she was dark like a negress, what? he was Charles Baudelaire, high on opium, her body fragmented, looking like his dead mother Rose and his dead sister Oona, they had buried all the family that morning in the yard, breaking wooden crates to make gravestones for their heads, it was chilly as the first winter cold set in, there was not any electricity, so at first they slept in the bed together solely for the animal warmth they generated to each other, but after a few days, they realized they were the only ones left, he held her unlike any woman he had held, nervous with his desire, he poked around her tight cunt, letting fly with the sperm, they waited silently in the room for nine months, the child coming out, he wore a mustache, had the feet of dog, eye of snake, eighteen pounds two ounces on the makeshift scale they made with levers attached to the lilac bush in the backyard, the blossoms dead, Leland placed stones in one bucket and the baby Luke in the other, figuring each stone for a pound, he measured eighteen on the scale, as the tanks continued to patrol the streets, they knew them to be electronically controlled so that no humans were in them, it took Sam and Leland awhile to accept this fact, as they fed Luke from the canned rations they had saved in the cellar, he spoke from the day he was born, being Mackool's nephew and son, he bought him two presents when he turned six months, a Luger and a cap gun, leaving the decision to him, whether he wanted illusion or real violence, he chose pageantry in the cap gun, constantly assaulting his mother as she breast fed him (her tits had bloomed after the birth of her first child), Luke fired a round of caps, making me jump for the sky, he said:

"Hands up, motherfucker," chewing on his toothless gums, he made a sucking noise like an old prospector.

Sam instead is thinking about Deirdre, that if she doesn't stop eating Christmas candy, she's going to blow up, already ten pounds overweight, Sam keeps telling her she's going to wind up like Leland in the cellar, so fat he can hardly move, but she's reconsidering, that's not a good thing to tell a little girl, but looking at that belly, Sam pictures her youngest sister pregnant, coming home to tell her daddy at her age, "the man in the candy store did it," with him coming in for the chorus, crazy kids crazy kids, you should have lived during the depression, Sam thinks of those long dresses then, that it wouldn't have been too bad, because her legs, the least attractive part of her, would be covered, she'd be on the corner of Delancey and the Bowery, selling apples, three for a nickel, how much would it take, she says, for Leland to leave her alone, a lifetime, and how to compute that in money, though bread has never been her concern, like her momma, she thinks that a larger presence always provides, a swami, she thinks, who brings fresh vegetables to the house each night, to sit cross legged on the floor of her head room, listening to the man talk in a mellow voice, the sound of her father and older brother disappears into the night, leaving behind a trace of whistling, as they are carried off on the wind.

But visiting for the holiday, Sam tenses with memories, sour thoughts of this house, knowing that her mother Rose is sneaking off this moment to the cellar, she had a bottle of vodka hidden in the washing machine, you'd think the father would let her drink with all the booze he slushes around his belly, Sam is high now, thinking, daddy is pregnant, he is about to give birth to Shirley Temple, "On the Good Ship Lollipop," electric ooze zapping the wave out of her kinky hair, and all through her youth, "you have naturally curly hair," mother Rose said, whenever Sam wanted to straighten out the matter, it was tight on her head, Sam thought of a dew rag, getting a conk, for it was that tight, brillo like, she ran a finger through it, but half way, it never happened differently, her finger collapsed on a snarl, she had a flash how she hated being a beautician, but did it so she could get out of high school, that's why she refused to see the musical *Hair* when a friend invited her to go for free, she danced now, looking at her face in the mirror of her head room, she let it glide, appreciating the sensual way the lower part of her body had sex now, though the top, she couldn't understand how the mother had a large bust, Sam had nipples, nothing else, though brown nipples that all her boyfriends liked, they were sensitive, responded to an instant touch, Sam thought of Jean Harlow, that she could have orgasms all day if she had a silk white dress like hers, braless, the cold smooth touch of the fabric on those brown nipples would drive her up the wall.

The Eye of God, she said, what would daddy say?

Oona told her that there hasn't been a night in the last two weeks when he didn't come home rocky, cursing, he says, "I don't like Sam going out with that O'Bromowitz," smart, pretending he doesn't know his name, it's Ira Wienstein, but daddy, he likes to blame his trouble on the Italians at the dock, the Jews in the grocery store, the Irish in the bars, never on his own head, he's a saint, spending his paycheck on his friends' drinks, most of them don't realize how many kids he has, O'Bromowitz, Stiletto, they called one of her boyfriends Lasagna, the worse thing Sam can think of would be to bring home the boy of her father's dreams, the boy of her nightmares, a skinny freckled redheaded guy named Clancy who works for IBM, wants to have a good Catholic family, she tokes hard on her hookah, it makes her so angry.

"What's going on in there?"

The old man is at the door.

"I'm just talking with Oona," Sam says, smiling to her younger sister who is zonked out.

"Open up this instant, Sam," he says.

"Please go away, daddy," in a nice mellow voice, she says, "I just got my period."

Gulp.

He moves off, humbled by the female chemistry, the word always makes him flush.

"Do you think daddy is good in bed?" Sam asked.

Oona smiled, by not answering, she told her.

86

"It must be like balling a walrus," Sam volunteered to break the silence.

They were back to their mother, who they decided was a great lover, white heat, a bundle of passions.

They were worried about her being drunk now, she even curses, which sounds funnier than, she never did that, Oona and Sam don't believe it, the words come out of her mouth foreign, she was drunker than she had ever been, partly because she had another miscarriage, and this time, without much fuss for anyone around her, she flushed it down the toilet, going about making peanut butter and jelly sandwiches for the children and their friends when they came home for lunch, it wasn't until after they left that she went into the cellar for the vodka, Oona found her in a heap of laundry, crying like a baby, she told her daughter what happened, Oona started to cry too . . .

She's gotten crazy with daddy never coming home to dinner, Michael never coming home to visit ever, whenever he calls, which is about once every two years, she gets drunk for a week, telling whoever walks in the door about her son who is a writer, and fifty-five years old now, she's no chicken, Sam doesn't understand why she's trying to have more babies, she won't be able to take care of them if they live and if they die like this one, X. Coole, she's a wreck for months, Sam told her to take it easy, that's when she started those curses again, not doing them properly.

"The fuck of hell I'll stop, the oldest daughter telling me that, I know you're after my husband."

It's not her usual tone, holy Rosey, which is dumb servility that everyone loves and approves of, a slave to this ship for the last thirty years, she should run out once just to see where the flock would go, this place falling apart if she did, it's not that she does any housework, Oona does all that, Sam before her, Sam can't remember a day where she's seen mother Rose vacuum, and making beds, she does her own half the time, the rest of the day daddy gets the sheets, throwing them over the bed, pulls them a little, and if it's a day off, goes directly to the bar.

"There isn't a person in this house that doesn't consider getting out of here the major focus of their life," Sam said to Oona.

"What about Leland?" Oona asked.

Sam was stopped, she toked on the hookah, exhaling a cloud of smoke in the room.

"He doesn't count."

Oona was thinking.

"It's impossible to bring a boyfriend home," she said.

"You should have seen what daddy did to some of my boyfriends," Sam said, grinning now, though it was bad then.

There was a knock at the door.

"I'll call the police, if you don't open up."

They put on a Stones record, loud, drowning out the Christmas noise outside.

You see, Sandra told Oona, it's alcohol violence that separates them from the older ones, she says, Mickey Mack Coole is the straightest one in this house, meaning he's pretty far gone too, but he's the watershed child between the alcoholic nation of mother and father, Leland & Emmett, though Patrick told Sam that he gave a bit of Sunshine to Emmett about a month ago, he says he's a preacher now, now a prophet, Sam doesn't understand Emmett, when she talks with him. Michael is stranger to

88

her though, but she's not a guy, even if the men in the house think that she is.

What Sam was saying was that Mickey Mike is the branch between the two nations of Coole, he was the first one to turn Sam on to drugs, after he got arrested in New Hampshire though, he got cold to the notion of people popping things, chewing them, shooting, smoking, he gets like the older tribesmen, drinking and talking about doom, another guilt ridden traveler, joyless, Sam feels a spark of fun, lighting out, it covers her body with the Joy of Coole, a happy smile on her face, she talks with Oona, she digs her, they are tight.

But the minute her boyfriend Ira thinks she's fooling around.

"You're doing that because you're unstable. That large family with all the brothers messed your head up," he says, because he took a psychology course at City College, Sam can't think that way, but home in the house for the holiday, memory colors gray, her momma is a drunk, one of those closet kinds, which is scarier, Sam tells Oona, than barrelhouse drunks like the men.

"Maybe we should turn her on," Oona says, but Sam says she'd act the same, it wouldn't help, because she sees things already.

You can't say the house has disintegrated because they have no religion, the house is filled with ghosts, saints, holy men from the past, Sam don't know what it is, though she's glad she's out of there, she wishes Oona could come with her, she's thinking, and Wolfe wets his bed every night, eleven years old, and Deirdre, she never stops eating, when she talks, her sentences never fit together, they don't make sense, Terry's going to kill daddy one of these days, if he hits him one more time, it's because they look alike, he used to do the same to Michael, daddy walks in the door drunk.

"What are you doing now?" he yelled, Michael sitting there reading, wham bam, and not lightly, no thank you mam, though all his drinking has poppa weakened.

The time he ripped up that story that Michael was writing, that was about ten years ago, Sam thought that was going to be the end of daddy, if looks could kill, daddy would have been dead a hundred times over from Michael, a thousand from Terry, but you try to understand, she tells Oona, say he is your father, that he's had a hard life, working overtime all the time, but he's irrational, never goes to the source of The Trouble, he picks out the first person available, one he knows won't attack in return, like a rat, Sam says, like a rat who eats his own, Sam is crying now, stoned out, pretty Sam, spaced out, she is high, crying in the stratosphere, big snowy tears, that fall on this house white, white like inner thigh, Sam is above the house, it is a doll house, with one side of the house opened, she moves the father to his room, locking the door, she places the other dolls around the dinner table, a two inch plastic turkey in the center of the table, nine dolls at the dining room table in her doll house, they all wet their pants, she is crying.

"He's cheap and dishonest, Oona," she says to her sister, who gives her solicitude by patting her back, putting her arms around the oldest sister.

Selfish, selfish, she says to herself.

The children be damned, she can hear her daddy saying in a bar, as he orders another round for the house.

He'll get drunk, get his supper, pass out on his plate, a

chicken leg in his hand, later when they venture down-stairs, there is a lull in the cacophony, he is snoring on the couch, disappointed that his son isn't in the nut-house, but only his two truant half sisters, the closer a tragedy is, the better he seems to feel, Sam's hated that aspect of being Irish, their sense of doom, though she thought herself Italian because people mistook her for a bambino, she was dark, short, stubby, but never fat, her legs were horsey, she's tried everything to improve them, Sam tells Oona, who has a perfectly shaped body to her small size, but since high school her legs swell up, she'd be out for a drive with Johnny Stiletto, after she finished work in a beauty parlor, they'd be out late.

When she got home, the dishes from supper were cleared away, though still not washed in the sink, she'd do them before she went to bed or the bugs feasted from the garbage, but before she even walked in the house, her daddy saw her getting out of the car, he ran out, shaking the door, pulling her out, "if she's pregnant you'll pay for this with your wop ass," he said to Johnny, Sam was embarrassed, she kissed the guy once all night, but Sam was desperate for anyone to hold her, she didn't care whether the hands were filled with grease in the cracks of his palm, that his nails were perennially dirty from car sludge, that he spoke in monosyllabic gas sta-tion English, *Your love is like a shining hubcap,* she once wrote, the first line to the only poem she ever wrote, *that spins along the thruway to my heart,* it con-tinued, *I hear the gearshift going, the gas pedal floored,* she thought, as her father pulled her by the arm, pincers his fingers were, *the wheels will spin & spin forever, my love, my Johnny Stiletto,* but then she thought, why doesn't he run daddy over with the car, we'll drive to California in a big stolen car, I'll be Sophia Loren, he can be Sal Mineo, oh Stiletto, let those snakes on your arms bite my father's tongue, stick his body under the radiator, the antifreeze covering his body like the coating on a new born baby, she wanted to hold a baby that came from her body, but in her room later that night, she pictured the child with tattoos on his arm, garter snakes instead of cobras like his father's, and toothless, sucking on her tit with its gums, it would be a boy, she'd call him Arnold, but terribly fucked up because she has no tits, Sam thinks about herself back then, with a nice round ass like a croup of a horse with those fat legs that used to swell up, she'd wear dresses like Kate Smith, she thought, when she grew up, but slim, an olived skinned beauty from the Mediterranean, Contessa Sandra Bologna, waiting for her boyfriend to come out from under his car so they could go to the movies, Contessa Sandra Napoli waiting for her kinky hair to unfold the tight curls, a straight haired dark eyed beauty, she was bound for Corfu, after she finished teasing the hair on this lady from Roslyn, smelly dead roots of these matrons, they kept telling her how nice it was to see a young girl learn a profession, dying their gray hair a wanton yellow, giving bobs to a lady who slept with every delivery man that entered her block, she was telling Sam about fidelity, "don't trust any of them," she said, telling her about the ignobility of manhood, "they're all cheats, honey, you leave them before they leave you, that's my motto . . ."

Sam tried to think what her motto was?

SEMPER FIDELIS.

Contessa Sandra ai Romano showed a customer the

underwear department, escorting them past her own cos-
metic counter, she was making eighty-five smackers a
week, the most she'd made in her life, the other job she
had was a maid in Old Westbury, you'd think the old
man, well, he was speechless, growing back to his tongue
this way:

"No daughter of mine is going to wait on the rich,"
saying the last word, pronouncing it like, scum.

It was coming to pass that they were all Communists
underneath the veneer of Long Island gentility.

"Being a nurse was an honest profession," mommy
said, "and my family had a maid before my father lost
all his money, but my own daughter . . ."

Nobility, a revolutionary elite, *milicianos,* armed peasants, the landed gentry . . .

"Filth, degradation, perdition, humility," Leland said,
warming up to his oration.

Sam finally had to quit.

At night daddy promised he'd get her a job on an
ocean liner, "they always need beauticians, you're a
lucky girl to be traveling around the world," he said, as
though she'd made the global tour already, another one
of his dreams, because he got things out of the kids that
way, promising, "I'll get you a job on the ships if you're
good," like a threat, because he knew too how badly
they all wanted to get out from under, the only one he
got papers for was Michael, he'd come home each night,
the old man, talking about how he met his son a few
weeks ago, going through customs, he says never again,
he does him a favor, "he winds up being a dope addict,"
he thought Michael was on smack, but spaced behind
whatever it was, Sam knew that Mick didn't use drugs,

and once daddy got Emmett a job after he bailed him out of jail for the nth time, the old man loved his sons when he had to bail them out of jail, going down to the station, he'd sign the papers for release, talking with the cop about civil service benefits or the need for a stop sign at an intersection, he'd go off, hitting every bar on Jericho Turnpike, telling the bartenders, proudly:

"I just bailed him out of the can, my second oldest, how you like them apples?"

Emmett bathed in alcohol that day, but that night, home in the house in front of his wife, Inspector Coole sings differently.

"An absolute disgrace, a mark upon your dear mother."

Sam wanted to come home, bailed out of jail for whoring around the bus depot, she wondered what he would do.

"My daughter," he'd say, proudly, to the bartender, "she's one of the best ten dollar throws on Long Island."

The two oldest male bears had to come up with their gloss when Sam came home from a date, Leland was the worst, giving his fantasy exegesis about what happened, he'd grab Sam or Oona, even Deirdre once, Sam thought that maybe she should have let him take a piece so he could get over being the fattest, oldest virgin in and out of Coole.

"He get much tonight?" Lee said, at first playful, but when he got started, it was *loco*.

"Did he touch you there?" goosing her ass with his fingers, hard, leaving a bruise on the cheek.

Daddy followed with his vaudeville act, asexual

94

though, for he seemed frightened at the suggestion, he was concerned about the social implications.

"What do the neighbors think with a young girl coming home at two in the morning with that crazy guinea driving that car without a muffler?"

Sam never answered, then he'd slap her, taking off his belt, he'd chase her around the table, then she'd see a break, fake to the left, he'd fall for her move, being drunk and off balance, Sam shot upstairs to her room, glad that she hadn't drunk so she didn't have to pee, she fell asleep with her heart pumping frantically.

"You'll have to come out sooner or later," she heard him yell in the hall, mommy waking up and asking what the commotion was for?

He yelled at her:

"You keep out of this, this is between me and my daughter," saying it like I wasn't her daughter, if I was his.

"She's getting too big for you to tell what to do," mother Rose said.

"No women is too old to be told what to do," he'd say.

Sam's making that up, for the old man never said a complete sentence or proclamation like that in his life.

His delivery was more like this.

"The guineas are taking over the waterfront and my own wife has to serve me meatballs for dinner."

It had to be negatively ethnic or he wouldn't say it.

His speech was never pastoral, that the day was beautiful, his children looked fine, his wife had on a nice dress.

95

Only one man ever lived in Coole and had anything nice to say about women, Sam told Oona, because Oona wasn't born when he was alive, he came from mother's side of the family, the Greens, he was Uncle Bill.

"Because they are women, they are beautiful, there are no ugly ones," he used to tell the boys on the porch, where he slept when he stayed with the family at Coole, Leland and Emmett laughed, Sam could see Michael listened.

He had a bald head, he looked like a cross between Ken Kesey and Jean Genet, though when Michael made this observation to Sam, she didn't know what he was talking about, nodding agreement, she didn't want to ask who they were, figuring they were people who lived in Mineola, she continued to talk with Michael about Uncle Bill, she was saying the same things to Oona tonight as she had said to Michael a few months earlier in Manhattan.

Uncle Bill was a purser on a tanker, and to a child's mind, Sam told Oona, she thought of purses, which Mickey Mike told her was not too far wrong, he said, "most pursers are homosexual," where Leland would say, "fucking faggot," making it sound in his Aquinas way, evil, sinful, it was because Leland was a latent heterosexual himself, Sam thought.

But about Uncle Bill.

The porch where he slept was damp and filled with Leland and Emmett in one corner, Michael in the other, when Uncle Bill was not there, and though the room reeks of alcohol sweat now, it's impossible to remember how nice it was, when Uncle Bill came to visit her, for Sam thought in her Shirley Temple way, they would marry, that he came only to see her, he was a stranger to the others, now the room, when Oona walks into it with Sam, smells of delirium tremors, Emmett's rotting stomach, a room of festering, cankered, a boil about to break, wounded, the walls pierced with a miserable sword, turning the room to a cell, it didn't used to be that way, Oona.

Mother Rose screams.

A bubble of wine coming up from her throat into her wine glass, she's awake from her jag, the old man must have told her about Eileen and Nora, Sam don't know much about the old man's side of the family, her mother came from a family of seven, but Sam doesn't want to talk about them, they depart again to the head room, placing a soft record on the stereo, she locks the door, Sanctuary, a place in turn of tastes and smells that has come to mean safety, she unravels her mind, folding out the edges where the story of her uncle lies, she's giving to her sister Oona, like a Christmas present, a man's life who remained good and kind to her, even after he had skin contact with the debilitating disease called Coole.

What she remembers is, the girl across the street talking about Korea the day Sam found out her uncle had died, she walked onto the porch, the walls covered with drawings, carvings, because her mother didn't like to scold the children for writing on the walls, though now she was sitting in the head room, emotions exploded in Sam tonight, ideas making her head pregnant with old traumas, Bill Uncle Bill, Sam keeps running off from you.

"Pompous literary dribble," she hears Leland say outside the door, he's talking to himself in the mirror.

He's banging his head on the mirror.

"You try to make it all misery and sorrow," he says, Sam knows Lee's talking to an outside ghost, because he's like daddy, he can blame The Trouble on Florida, Michael, mother Rose, his friends, his old girlfriend.

But the real world, when Sam was young, it consisted of an Uncle Bill who rode tankers to the east coast of Africa, and once when he returned he gave her a Congolese franc, her greatest piece of exotica, she made a necklace with it last year for her own Christmas present, he was speaking to her about a giant wooden giraffe he was going to bring home the next time, but he didn't

Thrown overboard, Grandma Green says, "by an African medicine man who was addicted to morphine . . ."

He rode tankers.

Sam pictured him straddling a boat, like a rubber one in a tub, riding out into the ocean like a cowboy on his bronc, ride Bill, buck, he was her rider.

His watch ticked when he slept, it glowed in the dark, it was magic,

". . . never have to wind . . ." he said to Sam, one night peeking in on him, she thought he was asleep, then he jumped up, hugging her, his heart beating, hers beating faster with the fear and joy, the watch ticked through her back as he held her tight.

Fantastic rumors circulated through the house that Uncle Bill was going out with one of the Miss Rheingold contestants, the kids stuffed the ballot boxes in three grocery stores for her, Sam being jealous of her, she voted for another, the redhead with horse teeth, she won, they always do, Sam thought, glad that her uncle was back to her.

Even Uncle Bill agreed with Sam about her daddy, he was trying to teach him to drive, he said to her:

"He's hopeless, if he gets a license, there won't be a person safe on the road."

He predicted to the world what the worst driver in the history of that noxious machine was going to do.

"These nutty Jews with their big Cadillacs," the old man said. "These wacky kids with their convertibles." "These nutty ladies with their Volkswagens." "These . . . these . . . these . . . crazy, they drive me crazy . . ."

The old man was in a panic the minute he got behind the wheel, telling the kids to stop yelling, he was going to crack up if he couldn't concentrate on the road, and yelling, Sam once saw him jump out of the car, for no reason she could think of, it was Christmas time so he was in his special holiday spirit, and they were shopping for gifts in Hempstead, which they never got, because he said, "you're all so bad, I'm turning right home," but he jumped out of the car, pulling this man twice his size from the seat of the car in front of him, he bashed the man in the mouth, then took his head, he kept hitting it on the roof of the car until a cop came.

They never arrested daddy, Sam said, because he had official badges and papers and stamps from the U.S. Treasury Dept., Inspector Coole never got his lumps like his children.

He dropped us at home, then went off to do his own Christmas shopping, it was like this:

The old man walked in the door, he had bundles under his arms from Christmas shopping, never any good stuff, his favorite place to shop was Horn & Hardarts, mommy would ask him to take Patrick out for a pair of shoes, he'd return home with day old cakes, cupcakes, cookies, tea biscuits, moldy and inedible from Horn & Hardarts, and when no one ate them, he screamed about us being ungrateful.

"When I was your age," he said, holding up a blueberry muffin with a fungus growing on it, "I would have done anything in the world to eat a cake like that."

No one believed that he was ever their age.

Wolfe spoke up.

"Would you jump off a building for one?"

But true to his style, he hit Terry for what Wolfe said, for he never touched the seventh son, being superstitious, being wise here.

Uncle Bill bought all the kids ice cream, so they didn't mind the moldy cakes.

"Your daddy's brogue is a durable oxford shoe with perforations," he told Leland, which made sense to Sam even if she didn't know what he was talking about, that good old watch kept ticking on.

"All women are beautiful," Sam keeps hearing her Uncle Bill say, he is home from the sea tonight, she's telling Oona, she can feel him in the room, he kisses her neck, "all women," she heard him say it throughout high school, when she had those swollen ankles, her flat chest, "all . . ." There are too many people in this House of Coole . . . "beautiful . . ." All of them, he told Sam, he whispered to her the day he left, telling her he'd be back in a month with a wooden giraffe, it would fill up the entire yard, using it as a slide for the children, Sam's lighting a joint, she's popping a pill, she wants that

Christmas tree to glow for her, just once, she wants, Oona, Uncle Bill to walk in the door with that giraffe outside in the snow, it'll be as tall as this house, Sam's sure of the size, and not Leland, daddy, any of them can stop her from sliding down it, glide down the neck, she is a lady, I'm fucking Uncle Bill under the wooden animal, Oona, she says, she's a lady because her ankles aren't puffy, her breasts, they're not like mother Rose's, she don't think they ever will be that size, but her kinky hair, she digs it, that nap, she likes it this moment losing her fingers in the knots, but later, she will pull it back tight on her head, making her look like the Contessa Sandra di Giraffe, it's Christmas in Coole, the family, she keeps thinking, she flashes, of Charles Manson, The Family, daddy riding around Death Valley with a shotgun, waiting for the revolution, Leland taking a turn through the sand in a dune buggy, Uncle Bill putting the giraffe in the middle of Charlie Manson's yard, "here's the answer," he says, smiling, because it is Christmas in the desert, feel the heat, Oona, Sam's getting a rush, there's going to be colors, up and down their faces, the spine tingles, each voice melting into the lights around the tree, The Family, oh Uncle Bill, Princess Sam says, I hear your watch ticking, it's inside her chest, Oona, look at the walls move away from us, it's Christmas, Michael's coming home tonight, Sam gets that vibration that he's coming to the flock, Leland be the Good Shepherd don't fuck up unmercifully again, and mother Rose, you can't be Monster Rose for us, we dig you Rosey O'Coole, hang loose baby, the rest is simple, The Trojan Giraffe with Helen of Coole played by Sandra, that big giraffe in the backyard for the kids to slide down, a wooden one, from the East Coast of Africa, painted yellow, painted orange, I'm spacing Oona, out, I'm flying, the rushes pour over me, *Erin Go Braugh,* Mr. Giraffe, my name is Sandra, I like my name, listen to that watch tick . . .

CHAPTER SIX

Michael sat that minute on Canal Street, plump, chubby, soft, and well stuffed on a milk crate in his brother Pat's storefront studio, twenty dollars a month with the back floor missing so the rats could watch him paint. "I have to sleep upstairs," Pat said, pointing through the hole in the ceiling, "because of the mice and rats." He was a younger brother, quiet, short, wiry, Patrick was considered the longshot in the Coole house, being left back twice, he had a mix up of the family traits, blond hair like Emmett, short like Oona, quiet like Michael, "but a slow learner," his teacher told mother Rose, figuring he wouldn't amount to more than less drunken than his brothers and sisters, he disproved this by taking acid (the only person in or outside Coole who has fared well with this drug, Mackool thought); it opened his nose, as they say, his head opened up wide to learning, and caught up in painting his last few years of high school, Patrick received a scholarship to art school, and now out of school momentarily, and now in the abandoned building on Canal Street, he was dealing, and arrested, nothing new for his family, Michael hadn't seen Patrick in many years, the last time being when he first came to New York for art school and stayed with his brother for the first month, they were hashing old stories, hashing through the pipe, smoking grass, getting high, striking a chord between them for what they had mutually survived, it was good not to be home, they decided, though sitting there stoned in New York together, their favorite and most consistent topic, as was true whenever any other combination of brother and brother, brother and sister, sister and sister, sister and brother met, they talked of their tribe, the usual way the conversation went was one Coole trying to outdo in depravity the other Coole with a story about their, what they called, Family.

"The old man called me a while ago," Pat said, taking a drag on the reefer, then passing it to Mackool. "He said you were in Bellevue."

"Bellevue!" Michael Mack said, astonished.

He looked confused at Patrick.

The younger brother was being quiet, calm Patrick.

"Don't worry, it's really Eileen and Nora they've got."

What was he talking about? Michael thought maybe Pat was giving an acid flashback.

"Who?"

"Our aunts, man. Emmett found out where they were living and paid a visit. It was under the Williamsburg Bridge."

Pat's interest in them being, he wanted to move into their building, when he heard how cheap the rent was and how fucked over the ladies were, Emmett told him they were due to leave this dimension moments away for the world that Jesus promised them on Earth, a life after life, what? Patrick said that Jorge, Quif's husband owned the building.

"So that's what he did with the inheritance!"

Pat asked Michael to explain what he was talking about.

"The inheritance, you remember, how Jorge managed to get the building when Grandma Coole died."

Before Grandma Coole died, her leg had to be amputated, or maybe it always was amputated, Mackool or Patrick can't remember this detail, for she hobbled about her apartment in a strange way, whipping up her cloth print dress at the window to the banana man, Mackool can remember that she never wore underwear and stuck a dark green salve on her ass, but he never found out why, she'd be off in the kitchen making heavy Irish pancakes she called boobalas, and telling him he should not play with the bad niggers down the block, for the good ones lived next door, because their father was a minister, which didn't endear him none to Grandma Coole, but from the West Indies, they had perfect British accents, and to her who despised the Irish worse than plague, they were the ultimate in grace and charm with their manners and gentle English ways, while her daughters Quif and Quim, the notorious Eileen and Nora, they didn't know what they were or cared to find out, it appeared, they simply were there at her funeral, because there was nowhere else to go that day; Nora not out of the house in fifteen years, her skin awful colored in sunlight, blotched and burned, translucent like a boneless white fish wrapped in newspaper, and this was before her body really went offal after it burned up in the cellar fire; Eileen had her Jorge, she was living the last months the other side of the street and down the block a ways from her mother, who—

"You keep that greaso from my door," she said to Eileen about her new find in the sweater factory, and then Augusta, Pat's godmother, was off raving about Eileen cutting out of the apartment, "she took my skirts, the fucker, when I get my hands on her, I'm going to—"

"They've come to get us!" Nora grated.

"Who? Who?" Augusta asked.

"They," she said. "They've come now!"

But it was Grandma Coole's funeral, this humid day on Rockaway Avenue, Jorge was crying, the father was silent and respectful, a champ at funerals, he missed his calling, and dressed in black, the suit was a government one he had, when the inspectors wore black suits, he looked like an undertaker, only blowing his front by wearing white cotton socks, Jorge was in a bright lavender suit, Eileen in and Nora out the door for a piss, it was the only things they did proficiently, while Aunt Augusta hacked, smoking her Pall Mall, which were later to do her in along with her drink, Mackool stole one from her pocketbook and gagged on it outside.

Jorge had a nervous habit of shaking his right leg, pushing up on the toes and bending the leg at the knee, kind of an exaggerated shuffle like a 1930's jitterbug, standing on the street corner in a checkered suit and swinging a watch chain while swinging his hips, though the suit was lavender and the watch was in hock, the chain was a string of paper clips; he did his dance the whole time the funeral went on, putting the cortege off their death rhythm as the honor guard, Jorge one of them, carried the coffin down the stairs.

"Get those ants out of your pants or walk behind us," the father Coole said.

Jorge ignored him, saying:

"They should at least have music, *verdad?*"

"That'll come afterward," the old man said, not sure of the last thing Panaqua The Latin said, bird dad, it sounded like, the old man didn't like the sound of it, feeling his heritage, he planned to get smashed after they got this stepmother of his in the ground.

And after that, after the funeral, the Irish wake, the drunken party, and several months later, came the will. Jorge got everything. "It's foul play, I tell you," Inspector Coole said, and before they could figure what Jorge did, he packed Quif and Quim, he split, Augusta dying a few months later of cancer and alcohol, the apartment building was sold, and the next time the father saw these folk again, was this night that Pat and Mike sat talking about it, the first time since the old man had heard from his sisters in those many years away from their dear brother. The last time Patrick and Mackool remember seeing Eileen and Jorge was a few months before Grandma Coole died, and they had stopped by Leland Coole's pad, Eileen with her husband and their black daughter Consuela Siobhan. They told mother Rose the baby was a neighbor's they were taking care of, but whenever Con Siobhan got hurt, fell on the floor and scraped her knee, crying:

"Momma, momma, I cut myself."

Eileen tended to her needs, if not like a mother, then at least like the source from which this hurt animal sprung.

The day Eileen first brought Jorge out to the Coole home, King Jorge took care to show the old man the cultural differences in their lives, the mother Rose eating it up because it had to do with her breasts, which she had a good pair of, considering that she nursed nine plus of them into poverty, Mackool would say they were 36 D, give or take a cup size, though he's sure no one except maybe counting that time their Uncle Al grabbed them at his sister Sam's first communion, what? The grope that day was done more in the spirit of celebration than in the actual lust mother Rose exuded, but that night with Jorge The Latin (¡*que kalor!*), his *corazon* afire, he was turned on and around by the momma, and kept hugging her to show his appreciation thereof, he grabbed a handful, and she hadn't that much attention in years.

Señor Panaqua, he said he was a blood relative of Columbus, as one of the kids, Emmett, skinny and ghost white next to the señor, E. said that the father of our country was Italian; with Jorge, gives him a quarter to beat it the hell out of here, screw up the man's form, he think, this child with his manners, "don't be so smart, see, *mira*," he said, with Emmett: "Mirror? What's he talking about?" And Emmett's father: "I don't know, but I don't like it." The señor pinched Emmett's ass, hard, and giving him a quarter, he moved toward the mother Rose now, his hair slicked back, his white on white shirt dirty with engine grease, because "the foecking Buick broke down on Northern State Parkway." The father didn't dig his language none, Jorge's hand moving toward the mother's blouse, while Quif, rather, er, Eileen, sat talking to no one about the girls in the factory, "Agnes got pregnant last week and she's not even . . ." The father going all different which ways and what, telling Eileen not to talk like that with the children in the room, as if they didn't know what she meant with three of them to a bed at night, added to complications, "Keep your hands off her, Jorgie," (pronouncing it oorgie) the father called, yelled, screamed, no, not screamed, blatted out, not like a fog horn, but not like a human voice either. Though it seemed that the mother Rose was delighted with the attention, she kept saying how romantic Spanish men were, Jorge's gold capped teeth agleam for her, engine grease on his white on white shirt and his silk lavender pants with his nose picker shoes pointed in mom's direction, his Buick 6 was parked out front, which had the old man uptight, yes he was once again incapable (his emotions were they to surface ever had to be doled out always in the absence of, rather than the presence of, and thus) incapable of getting tight from the beer in front of him, the young brother Patrick was saying:

"Hey, Jorge, where'd you get those mudflaps and that squirrel tail on the antenna?"

Jorge was pleased with the attention his machine was getting.

"Park that goddamn car in the garage, I don't want people to think it's mine. There's no excuse for this."

But mother Rose was into the action that day.

"Why don't we all go for a ride in it?"

But Jorge liked morphine, that is, he told Eileen that he did, and she thought, "why would anyone take it, if they didn't like it?" Jorge told Eileen he had to take it because he got shot in Korea, his left side really was missing, that wasn't a lie, but he told the parents that he came over to this country toward the middle fifties, and five minutes later talking about his boyhood in the Bronx after he came over from Cuba, catching himself with, "my family once visited the islands when we lived in Spain," though he needed his morphine now to block out the artillery he heard in his head, Quif black and blue on her arms too, and her carrot orange-red hair frazzled, because Jorge pretended she was Korean those nights when he had no money from her, he climbed the walls to China for a dropper of that, that, that . . .

No one had the nerve to call it what it was, the mother ascribing his behavior to his Spanish blood, the father to his Negro ancestry, the children not caring what his blood type was, they knew that he had come in louder than the old man to shut him for the afternoon, though they never heard the end after the Panaquas drove back to Brooklyn, Jorge leaving a 20 foot patch of rubber on the street, as he peeled out in his Buick 6, baby Con Siobhan waved goodbye to the children as the four different lights on his continental kit blinked *Va Con Dios*.

"If I hear anymore noise, I'm not buying that tree next week," the old man said, as his black-PR-Irish relatives pulled away. There hadn't been a sound for the last fifteen minutes, there wasn't going to be a sound for the rest of the night.

He was out of his chair, this a rarity, for he was this time after Patrick, a possible momentary blindness making him think it was Michael or Emmett.

"Who's the trouble maker this time?"

It appeared to be him, but no one had the nerve to say it, they just

Vanished!

Under the tables, one opened the window and jumped into the yard, Mackool made it out the backdoor and around the corner to the candy store, garbage pails were thrown in his path to stop his march, but to no avail, he ultimately caught one of them, to thrash, bop upside the head, kick the shit out of for his sad, lonely, sorry, fucked up, narrow head, as he thought, hitting one child and then another across the face, in the stomach, over the buttock with a thick, three sided ruler, he thought, why should I have a Puerto-Rican-Nigger for my broth-er-in-law? A question he didn't ask to humans, but to the lord above, who the father knew for Irish Catholic, if not from his very own neighborhood in Brooklyn, cer-tainly a god with florid skin, freckles, and ideas about order to make you think once be you dark skin, mighty tongued, blah blah, etc. etc. "She married a booger," he said to Leland. "She married a coon," he said to Em-mett, as Michael, prior to being hit for what he was to say, said: "Maybe he's Indian." And for this was given no supper, thank God, thank God, the boy thought, going to bed peaceful without potatoes and Wonder Bread in him, for that was all he ate, except peanut butter and marshmallow fluff.

"Wait until you see what's in your Christmas stocking, you wacky, crazy kid!"

Back in the old days, the old man's family, his three sisters, his stepmother, his father were all considered wacked out wacky, except him, because he managed to skip town before those carrot twins got him, where he split to Washington D.C., and got himself what he thought was, it was a good job, civil service, U.S. Customs temporarily until he made money to go to college in order to become the American ambassador to Ireland, security and fringe benefits, married to the little lady across the table from him now, who keeps insisting that his half sister's husband is Spanish.

"What about Aiman de Valera?" the second son Emmett The Blond before he became The Beast asked, he kept prodding his father, who didn't want to know from no de Valera if he was the King of Ireland.

"I tell you, it's a disgrace how that Eileen carries on. There no . . ."

"Excuse," Leland Jr. said.

"There isn't," Leland Sr. said.

"Quif and Quim," Michael said, the namer of the ladies, and was promptly wacked over the head with a newspaper for the wit shown.

Nora at least had her excuse, being her twin sister and cut from the same rare coin, she was declared incapacitated long years before, and Leland, Emmett, and Mickey Mack can remember staying at Grandma Coole's apartment for a summer vacation, and at night to have to sleep with Nora, because there were no beds, and none were worried about one of her nephews seducing her, since she still thought her cunt was where you peed from, although the boys never minded her monosyllabic nonsense of, "don't answer the door, they're coming for me," she'd say, whenever a kid on the block rang the bell for Leland, Emmett, or Mickey to come to play; Nora under no circumstances left that apartment, and

Grandma Coole to her daughter Quim Nora, "I'm crippled so you can't expect me to fight them off all the time for you." The two remained within doors and fought who was going to turn on the radio or flush the toilet, while Eileen was off getting laid in the backroom of the sweater factory she worked in, and Aunt Augusta, their half sister and the father's step sister, she was thinking about when her boyfriend Tansy was going to take her to a hockey game at the Garden.

Meanwhile, light and heavy years away in an apartment on Canal Street, a storefront studio that Patrick lived in and his brother Michael was visiting, they spoke of these things old and new, the past revisited with their words, and their thoughts wondering about to figure what would come of their aunts. The nostalgia grass had Patrick's mind pumping for one good Christmas, just a day in his life where he opened a dinky present and smiled like every other brat on the block; he was stumping for that one piece in his brain that could link a moment of happiness with his young world, the one he happily punched out of when he was fifteen, for his first voyage through the Coz, high off the planet with LSD, Patrick mooned over his thoughts as his brother Michael sat peacefully in the corner stoned out of his what-you-ma-callit too, for Michael was neither a big doper or drinker, and spaced evenly in his invention, Patrick knew, or at least felt, that even though there were no words between them this count, Mickey Mack certainly understood what was running through his brother's head this time of year.

There was the mutual image in their narcotized skulls of the wind tearing down MacDougal Street, Brooklyn,

113

for Patrick had convinced the family to let him spend the holiday with Grandma Coole and her daughters, his god-mother Aunt Augusta, who promised a night at the Garden with her and her boyfriend Tansy, and Christmas day she brought out a present of puppets, which Pat loved then, and immediately tangling the strings, they broke. The noise his four relatives made was of an equal volume with the screams of his family's house on Long Island, he was at peace with men of good will, Nora telling Pat: "They'll probably take you too, when they come for me," and Eileen constantly leaving the living room, because she didn't like the program on the radio, she'd re-enter with a new sweater on every fifteen minutes, cashmeres, wools, banlons, stuffed in her large pocket-book each night she left the sweater factory, her breasts showed through the sweaters like nose cones, for she wore those pointed brassieres of the period that typified street essence, sex, and love. Patrick stood up and started for the other room for a leak, and while walking through the bedrooms of this railroad flat, he caught Eileen taking off her sweater, a nice pair of buns falling out of the bra she was removing. Pat's initial surprise was that he imagined her breasts to be shaped exactly like her bras showed them, i. e. nose coned, and when they fell from their cups round and pink with brown freckles and pink nipples, upturned underneath and sloped down from above, he got his first hardon, and almost understood what it meant, with Eileen taking it nonchalantly, she didn't seem disturbed that her young nephew's eyes were bugged out of his head and that the area around his fly stood up like a tent pole. He was going to touch one of the tits, but Eileen countered with, "Why don't you be a nice kid and take your piss." Pat stood staring at the well shaped boobs, and it was there that he first began to call her Quif, like Emmett and Leland did, though Nora remained Nora, Quimless since she was cuntless, sexless and alone with her horrors, her brain possibly peopled with saints' pudendums, though the real thing was not something he thought of her as considering in her bouts with the world coming to confiscate her body from this apartment. Nora had her monsters, Eileen Quif had not met Jorge yet, and Aunt Augusta had her nervous and scared boyfriend Tansy, an elfin printer whose hands were filled with printer's ink and too shaky to open his own beer, "can you open this for me," he said to Pat, and pop, the beer foamed onto the floor, with Nora jumping back at the site of the white froth, "Jesus!" she said, shaking, as though it were the frighteningest thing to happen in her life, it was, it was, she was the first speed freak that Pat had ever met, though she never touched drugs or alcohol, her nerves jangled on her arms like cufflinks, and you could hear her joints chatter as though they had no home in her body, and because Tansy was drunk too, he brought over mistletoe, and Grandma Coole kept trying for Nora to go under the weed with Tansy, catch her off guard so that Tansy could plaster her with a smudgy kiss.

"It's a sin to kiss a man you're not married to," she said to the group, shooting from the room in a flush and rattle, while Eileen was in the bedroom with a new sweater, red, very tight, Tansy kissed her instead; she was fighting him off too, because if she did kiss him, as soon as Pat's godmother Aunt Augusta got drunk, which she did promptly upon returning home each night from the women's shop she worked in on Bushwick Avenue; she'd be drunk and complaining, "that prick is going to give me a stroke with the way he works me," referring to her boss Murrary the Hebe, Eileen called him.

Eileen was no dumb sweater girl flirter, she knew who to come on to where, do it at the factory, where the guy takes you to a movie after work and you go for a beer at Nathan's, you don't mess with your sister's boyfriend, no matter how small and insignificant his body was in that drab gray suit, and those brown shoes, whew! Christ, he was no classy case to deal with, and shaking with his alcohol palsy, Nora in the corner cringing from what?, Grandma Coole produced a Christmas card from a deep drawer of the chest in the mysterious part of the apartment called the vestibule, and all Pat could think of were camels when she said that word with her lilting incoherent brogue, a secret cave in the desert, VESTIBULE, as Aunt Augusta choked on another Pall Mall.

Grandma Coole showed them the postcard she showed them every year, as Nora got up to walk into the kitchen, as Tansy snagged her under the mistletoe—she yelled—let out a scream that made you think he stuck his beer can up her; Aunt Augusta said Nora was saying that, meaning her scream, to get attention, and there was no excuse for that here, Gusty took the card from her mother, it was a picture of Santa climbing down the chimney without his pants on, a cock and balls so large they were slung over his shoulder like a bundle filled with gifts, it read:

Twas the night before Christmas
And all through the cathouse

Not a creature was stirring
Not even a louse . . .

Stanzas, Pat didn't know what half the words were, but they laughed hard in a way he knew the old man wouldn't approve of, and this made him feel well, to think of his father out of sorts with these gals, as though the old man's own boyhood was bad enough in a house of redheads, he had to marry a pretty scatter brain from Brooklyn, who casually talked him into the idea of having nine plus children, specifically, one blue baby, four miscarriages, countless takes and false starts, all under the malevolent aegis of love and marriage.

"We're going to the hockey game tonight at the Garden," Augusta told Pat, putting her lipstick on in front of the dining room mirror, standing there in her slip and bra, and Tansy nervous in his shakes, he'd ask her to put clothes on, while the kid's in the room; she told him and whenever she does, he shuts up, this timid man with his finger nails dirty from printer's ink, "he likes to look, which is more than I can say for you. You got no excuses. Besides, I'm his godmother, don't you think I get more liberties because of that?"

"I'm not going to argue with you, Gusty, when you get like this."

"Get like what?"

She looked good in her tough redheaded way, dressed nicely because she worked in the dress shop, or here, in this case, undressed nicely in her underclothes, since she was a slim, tall woman with still a good figure and appeal.

"Just because I'm feeling good, because it's Christmas

117

and my nephew is here. You're becoming a real dipso-
maniac, Tansy, can't you hold the suds lately?"

"I can hold it. Now don't get me angry or my gland
will hurt all night and I won't be able to enjoy the
game."

"You and your gland. When you going to learn that
things called a cock and not a gland?" she said, looking
defiant, monkeyish in the way her mouth set below her
high cheekbones, and her red hair seeming to go on fire
when she got into a rage.

"You don't have to talk that way with—" pointing toward Patrick, who knew Tansy had forgotten his name;
Tansy mumbled a word that sounded like Frank, then
added, "here . . ."

"I'm going to hang you by that gland tonight, if you
keep bugging me with your crap," she said, as she fum-
bled in her pocketbook for mascara.

Skinny, runty Tansy looked smaller in rooms with Augusta around than he did anywhere else in his day. At
the print shop he was a minor celebrity, because his father was once the head of the shop, but near her, the
nearer he came to know he was dribble; he was a small
man, older than her, and Patrick loved to stand next to
him, because he was short himself at ten or twelve years
old, and still he nearly held ground with Tansy, who was
a hair taller than Augusta's nipples, and when they
danced, which they loved to do when drunk, he usually
rested his tired head on her breasts, and she would stroke
his balding head as though he were her babe; he was
older than her, a nondescript florid face, the man sitting
across from you on the Canarsie Line train, he mur-
mured his apologies to her:

"I'm sorry, I just thought—"

"Drink, don't think," she said, and drunker, each time Pat went to a hockey game with them, she was drunker until the end, when he visited her on her death bed, the pack of Pall Mall still next to her bed.

"Somebody give me one last fuck before I go," she yelled in the hospital, delirious, and the father Coole shooting his children out the room.

"She doesn't know what she's talking about," he said to Patrick, but he knew her too well to believe that.

Tansy was still at her.

"Can't you slip into a robe before we go?" he asked.

"I'll let the world see everything!"

And she did.

She pushed him out of her way and ran up to the boy, ripping off her bra and raising up her slip, she didn't have underwear on.

"See what your auntie's got, Pat!"

A red hot snatch and pair of the finest boobs in East New York, he thought.

He blushed.

But he couldn't look away, for though she was in her late thirties, her dugs were fine, a small hard pair of nubbins, well they knocked brother Patrick over, and that red hair on her bush looked warmer than, it got hotter looking with each eyeful in youthful succession, like a midget he was, small and horny for proxy incest, since they were not related by blood, and he was ten years old, she was a looker, something superfine to see, and the lust, his first, was like a stiff fiberglass sheet along his back, and his body covered with a patina of sweat, it was sinful, which made it worth it, and it was new, which made it worth more, and Tansy could see this ritual unfolding.

Her lover pulled on her arm, then he ran into the bedroom and came back with a terrycloth bathrobe that Eileen wore; he threw it around her, as she started to cry on his shoulder, he took her into the bathroom for a shower, and he was out in minutes, his red face beet color now, his nose like the blood vessels on the surface were to pop if she walked off from her shower naked again, because on the way in she protested that the robe was Eileen's, and that she wouldn't wear her crap ever. Tansy put his shakey hand on the boy's shoulder, placed a can of beer in front of him, then handed him a church key. "My gland, please," he said, pointing to his crotch. "I'm afraid it may herniate from the pressure on the can."

When Patrick opened the can, Tansy scooped it up faster than light, knocking Pat's hand out of the way, and spilled foam on his own musty gray suit with the wide lapels, the foam falling on the bright shine of his black cordovan shoes that riveted him to the floor, his face was re-flushed.

"She, had, too, much, to, drink," he said, neither pausing nor stuttering between each word, though the impact felt like that, in visual terms, his words were like bucked and gapped front teeth, if this ridiculous analogy be allowed. "She'll, be, all, right, in, a, few, minutes."

He patted the godson on the shoulder, walked into the living room where Grandma Coole, Eileen and Nora were watching television, oblivious to the noise that had gone down in the other room. That's the way it was, Pat thought. Augusta screamed from the bathroom; Nora screamed from the living room; Eileen screamed in the bedroom that someone had worn her terrycloth robe; Grandma Coole screamed for quiet so she could watch the program, blathering through her gums this incoherent English-American version of Irish, or vice versa, it was only Mickey Mack Coole, it was said in the family, who knew how to understand this enigma, since at a young age, she taught him how to swear in Irish, or whatever language it was she spoke.

"If you fucked her more," Eileen said to Tansy, "she wouldn't be so drunken crazy tonight."

"The gland," he whispered, patting his groin.

He sat down next to Quif, stop this! he sat down next to Eileen, patted her knee, not sexually, but affectionately, like one would do to a dog or cat.

"Too much to drink," he said. "She'll be all right in a few minutes."

Nora was sitting next to her mother, Nora was sucking on a crucifix.

Pat was at the dining room table, staring at his puppets, amazed at what he had seen, excited, he tried to imagine—not fucking with his two mouse puppets—but a semblance of sex, or what he thought it was like in his head, something where the strings tangled and they pressed so hard to each other, their spines cracked and their wooden heads fell off. "Let's fuck," he heard the male mouse puppet say to the female, and the V of her black underwear drove him wild with this new feeling for sex. Augusta can stay drunk anytime, he thought.

Tansy came back into the living room with Augusta on his arm. They were ready to go to Madison Square Garden, and they told Pat to find his coat.

Grandma Coole, Eileen and Nora wished them Merry Christmas, as they bundled up and walked to the subway station.

"Happy Nude Year too," Aunt Augusta called, falling into Tansy, who fell into Patrick, who fell down the steps, taking his godmother and her boyfriend with him. Augusta danced down the street zagging back and forth, falling into passerbys, leaning on telephone poles, making obscene noises to men in transit from their homes to church services, women on their way home from last minute shopping.

Once she got to the Garden her salty tongue grew larger and louder; call down hot dog men, people in front rows who didn't root for the Rangers, Gump Worsley, the entire Toronto Maple Leaf team, especially Canadians, she had an especial venom for them, her raven heart unwound, exploded, lashed out horribly. It was here her beauty became apparent, for to stay with her you had to love her deeply, which Patrick and Tansy did, but she was an embarrassment, and as colorful as she got, there was also the demented frustration of an older woman gone sour with booze and years unmarried, unfilled with love, the Garden was her dildo, she got off rocks here, and the words and curses flowed from her like a sebaceous orifice, her words like sanies, puscular and swollen with infection, a gangrene of vulgar sounds and emissions, she farted and belched, and even on occasion puked her catharsis, so she often left the arena in a sweat, her hair unkempt and mussed as by a violent swollen lover who came to her as aggressively strong as she was aggressively weak. "Come on, you Canuck asshole, watch the fucking stick!" Whenever a fight broke on the ice, Augusta's monkey red face took on a further animal calm and she slathered at the mouth, drooling out curses now like love sonnets, she cooed for blood and when she was given gashes on the ice, she melted as though by seduction into a pool of fermented spirits and fomented anger, her frustration dripped from her like tricklets of blood, and there was a holiness to her face that would frighten a ghost.

"Fuck it all, Sullivan," she yelled, her false teeth coming loose, she'd jam them back in her mouth and suck her tongue till it blistered. The buttons on her blouse popped, and she'd walk from the Garden in a state resembling raped; Tansy, he'd be paler than when he walked in, if that were possible for a man with the complexion of a bleached sheet (with red stains on his cheeks for his surfacing blood vessels), it appeared that the only time Tansy's gland activated was when the Rangers scored a goal, and the sight of these two lovers was a gruesome spectacle in violence as well as how they abused their minds and bodies with drink and fierceness toward each other, and as Tansy later went to the men's room in a bar, Aunt Augusta leaned to Pat, grabbed him forcefully and rammed her tongue in his mouth, pawing him, sticking her nails in his back till he nearly screamed for release.

"Pat, I'm a godmother who could fuck that entire National Hockey League in one night and still be hungry for it."

He didn't know what to say and shook his head.

"Don't just shake your head, I know you think I'm terrible."

He didn't answer.

"Don't bullshit me," she said. "I know what you think."

Patrick didn't know what to say, and she got worse defensively, pathological, until Tansy came back and pulled her off her godson.

"He's not bullshitting me," she said to Tansy, trying to lean over to slap Pat, who wishing he were home, no, that would be the same. He wanted nothing then, and sat absorbing her tirade.

Tansy would return from the john, picking his nose, and scrounged up inside himself. If he didn't pay for her dates, Patrick would have recommended she rid herself of him, but they had been going *steady,* for that is what they called it, for fifteen years, and once when you see them holding hands, kissing, they said: "Maybe we'll go down to city hall next week," though no one was fooled, especially themselves, there was something in them that denied the institution of marriage and the institution of divorce, for that would be the only logical progression after a formal coupling, it was rebellion joined them Catholic anarchists all, God haunted their days, but they refused him homage, and hell was always near, it had to be that way, with heaven a bore and purgatory a bad promise, they were steady with each other, and that was the best way to describe their suspended state, a place where they held each other up and prevented the shakes from taking hold, steadier and steadier they became, stiffer, albeit less formal. "There's no excuse not to get married," Augusta said, and Tansy: "There's no excuse to get married." And sometimes the one would take the other's line and say it, while the other followed with the other's line, and repeated in a way to sound like they were both saying the same thing no matter who said what, they stayed as they were, and kept going steady.

There was this jar that Augusta kept in a closet in the kitchen, which would fill the first two weeks of every month with money saved for a wedding ring and a honeymoon, and about the middle of the month, for it never varied, Augusta and Tansy took the money out and got drunk on Broadway, go to Rockaway Beach or Coney Island, or maybe see a movie first then get drunk in Magees Bar, an Irish pub owned by the father of a former pitcher for the New York Yankees farm team, but always, and it would be breaking the highest commandment if they didn't, they'd have money for the Rangers whenever they were in town, which was another oddity, they'd go to every home game, but they refused to buy a season's pass.

"We ought to, there's no reason not to."

"We'll wait till next season. This one's almost gone now."

"Next season, then we'll have no excuse not to."

"None at all, yes."

After the game that night, one fight with the usher, who asked her to sit down, one shout out with a fan, her nylon stockings torn and stained with mustard and beer, her buttons still unbuttoned, and her winter coat thrown over her arm, they walked out to the street and passed through the crowd to a 2 shot for 50 cents bar. Augusta continued with her useless attack on Patrick and Tansy alternately, often calling down her boyfriend as though he were a bad godson and often shouting at Pat as though he were her lover. She forced Pat to drink half a glass of Irish, which he wanted to puke up instantly, the

125

burning in his windpipe still there after three ginger ales and a coke, his forehead burning, and sweating underneath his winter clothes, although he knew himself chilly. She leaned over to kiss Tansy and in her drunkenness, when she got within lip range, she forgot what she had come for and instead slapped his face, thwap! with the clientele looking annoyed at them, and hoping the bartender would 86 them shortly, which he did, after pulling and scraping Augusta through the sawdust and depositing her on the street, as Tansy kept trying to tip the man five dollars for Christmas, the bartender kept saying: "Keep you money, I don't need." "But I insist," Tansy said, with his face pained from his gland about to explode with the excitement.

On the street, Tansy insisted Augusta shouldn't have given Pat the whisky, for he was wobbling and bumping along without sense or direction. But flushing in his face, he apologized for criticizing her, and turned to Pat, saying the next bar he went with them, he would buy Patrick a drink, which was not what Pat needed. Tansy's hands fluttered about his face nervously, and Augusta kept saying he was a fag. "Can't you control yourself, Christ!" And he kept apologizing. It was an awful evening, the snow turning to slush and then to rain, Augusta going from exuberant to morbid, and Tansy apologizing for everything imaginable. Back at the apartment, the others were asleep, and when they bedded down to the couch, with Patrick sleeping on a cot across from them, Augusta tried to get Tansy to screw her, but he protested, my gland, my gland.

Patrick could feel her red hair giving off a glow in the

126

dark from her passions, she was rolling over Tansy and Pat could smell her heat.

"Don't Gus, Frank might see," for he still didn't remember Patrick's name.

Pat rapped his eyes tighter and prayed he might fall asleep, but it would not come to him.

He heard her body rolling, her moans more like a wounded cow then an empassioned woman. The muted silences from Tansy were worse, and Pat imagined Tansy's gland, whichever one it was, swelling and about to burst from the pain. "It hurts, it hurts," he heard him say. "Please stop, Gusty." But he could hear her torso flapping wet and half alive against the deadened shell Tansy lived in, and her sounds resembled the ecstacy of damnation. Patrick smelled tears and pussy juice, though he wasn't sure what the latter smell was, and he shrank lower and tighter into his blankets. The cold was working through his body like novacaine, and as he dozed off, he heard Tansy plead one more time for his gland, one more time that Pat may hear them, and then Augusta saying: "He might learn something if he is." There was the smell of Pall Mall cigarettes then, and then it was morning.

CHAPTER SEVEN

Mother Rose Coole should say, I want more wine, less children, none at all, or just little ones, she loves them young. After all she was a child nurse at Saint Vincent's Hospital. Greenwich Village, USA. When they grow up, they leave home, she never sees them except on holidays, fuck Jesus, fuck him, Mary, Mary, Mary; she's got to get sober before she go upstairs, and why did she get married anyway? Twenty-six years old, you're no chicken, breasts begin to sag, that is ridiculous, she was beautiful, like a young Barbara Stanwyck (Mackool's fantasy), a big bobbed hairdo that was the thing in the 1940's, and Leland Coole was handsome too in his Navy blues, while around the corner in their neighborhood in Brooklyn, there lurked Jackie Gleason, who was in love with Rose

Coole, he even made eyes at her twenty-five years later that time he sent Lee and Rosey tickets for a taping of a show, and then they went backstage afterward. They had never been backstage for anything, never in any theater, in high schools, in New York, on Long Island, nowhere. He even used, Jackie, her name in one of his bits for Joe the Bartender. "You remember Rose," he says to that syphilitic character drooling next to him, and then Joe goes off into that beautiful memory lane he always makes her cry over, all those Irish names he used from his old neighborhood, there were so many who loved her too. Oh, but there was tall Pugh, who became a sea captain on his own ocean liner, imagine that, and with a big white house in Sands Point, Long Island that she visited with her husband a few years back, and him kissing her when Leland went into the other room for drinks. The joy in those old veins! Who needs money with that joy? Money is not what she needs, and she tells the children that too, be poets, painters, anarchists, lovers, crazies, but never worry about money, for God (meaning the state) will provide, and that makes their father furious, he'll accuse her of drinking, when she talks like that, she has been drinking, yes she has, she has drunk herself shitty, Virgin Mary Shoe, the pig in her eye, the piss in her shoe, the holy mother sneaker, Mary, Mary, Mary, pretty white anglo bitch, why do they never assume your aquiline nose, your baggy breasts to fill Galillee with milk, she loves and prays to you each day, and you only visit her, how many times, just a few, a few simple miracles in her life, and her confessor tells her Rose must drink less, as though you had not come, that secretly the priests knew you were either a goddess or a whore, but never a real mother. Rose is so tired, she hasn't slept a wink. "Let me die, let me die," she blathers into the dirty laundry, but even inaudible to herself, she does not believe what she is saying, and should she go to confession the next day, this or her drunkenness shall not enter into her sins, for they are natural acts in this life, and her only repentance to God will be for not working harder for her husband and children. Leland, Leland, Emmett, Michael, Sandra, Patrick, Oona, Terence, Deirdre, Wolfe Tone Cooles. The dead ones not forgotten, like Aidan, Marie, Seamus, Oliver, Dawn. Her poor oldest, she thinks, sleeping over there in his bed, they hurt him in the Army, and for this the government will not take anymore of her sons. Her poor baby.

There used to be, before she got married, the maid to do her laundry, the maid to make the bed, the cook for dinner, and her father owned those beautiful horses. Her mother went to the best boarding schools, they had French blood, they did, and Rose's grandfather wrote for the biggest newspapers in the land, a pacifist and a bigamist, a grand father with his elegant suits and waxed mustaches. But she remembers somewhere saying all this, and does not wish to continue pitying herself further.

The Rose of Kennedy, and the Rose of Coole.

Her greatest love was a man named Sweeney Pugh. Her second greatest love was Aloysius Neeri. The third was Inspector Coole. There were no fourths or fifths; there were no second choices after the first and second left. There were the hawk eyes of Leland, and there was that semblance they call love. There were no birth control pills, and if there were, they would be flushed down the toilet.

"I'm a beatnik," she says to, who?

She says:

"Pugh, Pugh, Pugh, where will you be when I am gone?"

Sleep soothes her for awhile, and dreams do not enter into this sleep. She is dreamless, alone, phantom-like in motherhood, a little Catholic school girl playing hooky from her holy family.

CHAPTER EIGHT

Two princes talked silently; there was the cacophony below them, for they met in an attic. Like an engine, the voices below roared, the father initiating his traditional Christmas holocaust; this season it was about his sisters, though his conversation was impossible to decipher, and most who heard him still believed he spoke about his son Michael in prison or the glue factory or both. "Where is that mother now," he said. "Where did she disappear to?" His favorite other words followed, for instance, a wacky here, an Italian under the bed, a crazy now and then another shenanigan, World War, worry worry, Trouble, would he never be through with his catalog? No, for he was a man of tradition, and this was his style. The children were definitely not going to get presents this year, and yet they always found their gift under the tree, a tie, a pair of underwear, socks, one flannel shirt each, whether they were male or female, half of one and none of the other, AC/DC, straight, virgin or whore, stud or monk, the flannel shirt came down to them with the sacred way of God attached to each button, and they did keep you warm, they often were attractive, agh! they were ugly as hell were hell as ugly as this night were now; they never were enjoyable, they came with pain and inarticulate grumbles about what lousy, selfish bastards each child was to its (forget about his or hers) parent, and so the children often more than not preferred to stay bad and not be brought down with these gifts. Better still, Terence and Wolfe stayed in their attic away from the mess below, remaining aloof in their attic, and talking, like two princes, smoking cigarettes and sipping brandy Terence had an older friend buy for him this Eve, for Terry was but fourteen and his brother the Wolfe was eleven or twelve or somewhere around this age, both of them left back enough times in school not to be able to determine their age through the grade they attended.

"Do you still believe in Santa Claus, Wolfe?" his brother Terry asked.

The Wolfe had his mischievous look, which usually was backed by a recent prank pulled. The attic smelled of urine from the bowels of Wolfe Tone Coole, who pissed nightly in his sheets, the room like a public john in a bus depot from this smell, which had to do with the youngest son's faulty blatter. It went like this: "Now you're not going to wet your bed tonight?" "I promise." "You promise not to wet it anymore. You're too old to be doing this." "I promise." "It's not a healthy sign for a

boy your age to be wetting the bed nightly." "I promise
not to wet the bed." "Pray to God not to let you wet the
bed tonight." "I'll pray to God not to wet this bed."
"And promise not to do it other nights either." "Or other
nights either, I promise." "Or ever again." "I'm promising." "Do you really promise." "A promise is a promise,"
he said to Terry or his mother Rose, his father, sisters,
Leland, the dog, his picture of Saint Francis, to his baseball glove, to whomever he made the vow to that night,
"I promise," Wolfe said, and shortly after dosing off, the
vow was broken, the bed was wet, and in the morning,
he woke with his sheets the color of the Yellow River,
his mattress smelling that much stronger uric, his head
that much lower, he said to Terence:

"One good thing is that I don't have to go to the bathroom when I wake up, and can go right downstairs for
my breakfast."

Terence lifted two cement barbells, doing an exercise
for his lats. The window to the attic was open snow coming in the window the attic cold both them dressed in
their overcoats. The older brother continued his ritual,
flexing his muscles in the long narrow mirror at the end
of the attic, his image broken diagonally by a crack Wolfe
introduced to the glass that afternoon with his foot he
had the urge to put through the glass for the reason of
discovering what would happen, it broke. The physical
workout that Terence was engaged in was an arduous
procedure he performed each day in the attic for two
hours, the explanation being, "I'm going to get him yet!"
The epithet, if it may be called that, was directed at his
daddy, and the workout had to do with a vendetta Terence had toward this man, since the father had put this

boy through more shit and grief than a sun crazed Camp Lejeune drill sergeant could put a platoon of pacifists through in a swamp filled with alligators. Terence, you see, was the father's second ghost, the first being Mickey Mack, who also resembled the father in the face the way Terence resembled Michael, as both looked like the father, who looked like his sons, the ones he wished to wipe out, because their looks reminded him too much of his past, which he would as soon forget as be reminded about with his dumb sons there, like mirrors, like reflections, like twins, like anything but his sons.

Terence reminded his father of a forgotten past, when he was a lad bouncing his ball on those Brooklyn streets lonely, desolate, friendless . . .

But Terry had all the friends in the world, who he entertained in his attic, make out parties, beer parties, pot parties, heroin parties, fuck parties, many parties as long as his father wasn't at home. For when the father was home, the steps leading to the attic were too steep and the passageway too narrow for the father to venture there, and Terry never had to worry about the father finding out he had a party in the attic, as long as he had his parties when the father was not at home. Terry was the handsomest boy, and he had many girlfriends that the father would likewise like his daughters' boyfriends chase from the house rapidly, rabidly, his eyes aglitter with thoughts that his young son was fucking, which he was and which he enjoyed, and which his father thought: "Another son living in sin, oh God what have I done wrong to deserve this?" Italians, Jews, Blacks, Puerto Ricans, English, German, he knew, the father, that these kinds fucked early, but his own he felt should wait till

135

they were married, like the priests and nuns had taught them to. Then there were the sins of thought that the father had no control of, but which he knew his son to be actively engaged in, those thighs, cunts, tits, ass, those whispers, long breaths, sighs, he knew his son constantly thought of now. The Inspector was drunk with hysterical omissions here, and with his jumbled brain and his improper accent, he kept trying to figure, since he pronounced "taught" as though it were pronounced "thought," and "thought" as though it were "taught," whether he thought Terry did these things, or had he taught him not to do these things, or whether he was trying to mean thought when he wanted taught or was it vice versa? This was a problem. For had his own head been calmer this night, the father could figure whether when he said: "I taught Terry not to do that," he meant instead that he thought Terry not to do that, for the priests said that it was a sin either of thought, deed, or action, though when he thought or taught about it now, it could mean of taught, deed, or action, which to his mind, after finding out about his half sisters, made more sense, he taught, then anything else he taught that night, he thought. "I taught my children to be proper, what went wrong?" And immediately, he thought, do I mean taught or thought, for he taught he meant thought, though he might have thought he meant taught, or worse, that he taught Terry he meant taught, or that he thought Terry he meant thought, which has nothing at all to do with Terence and Wolfe in the attic, the one reading his brother Michael's letters, both love and otherwise, playing a conga drum that Emmett stole for them from a party their older brother told them, "thrown by a lot of rich Jews who will never miss the thing." There was also a three foot high styrofoam Lowenbrau mug that Terry and Wolfe used as a hamper, and as each thought, they equally taught one another not to trust their father, the older brother showing the younger how to use the weights effectively so that when the time was right, they would teach their father, should he punch Terry too often, which the father constantly did, there shortly would be hell to pay for this. Forgetting about Santa Claus then, for they were like other people in Coole, who never had a logical thought in their lives, they jumped to:

"Does the old man mean thought or taught, when he says either thought or taught," Terry said to Wolfe, who grinned back total lack of understanding.

They wrestled instead, and their father called up, as they rolled over the attic floor.

"I thought you not to be like this. I taught I told you not to fool around."

They laughed, they proceeded not to stop.

Then they tired of this, Terry going back to his barbells, and Wolfe looking through the hole in the floor that was directly above the toilet seat. Wolfe was laughing.

"What's so funny," Terry asked?

Leland was jerking off for the third time today, Wolfe said.

"Who wants to watch that. I'd rather see one of Oona's friends in there undressing into a bathing suit or something."

They both broke out laughing at this.

Terry watched the veins in his arms bulge as he said this. Pretty soon, he thought, the old man would get his lumps.

While the Wolfe's mind was on baseball, cigarettes, and how he felt high from the brandy he was drinking.

The attic they were in had changed greatly since Patrick last lived there and when Michael first lived there. Plasterboard now covered the walls, put up haphazardly on the slanted walls, by an unemployed plumber the old man knew in one of his haunts. The father collected these kind of men, who told him their sad stories late in the evening a few hours before the bartender shewed them out to the street, where with their arms about each other, not so much for camaraderie as to hold each other up, they wended to Mrs. Coole's boarding house, where the man slept on the couch and the father ventured up the stairs (careful not to step on the fifth step which creaked), crawled into bed with his beloved wife, who fixed breakfast for the man the next morning, the father telling him:

"Have you ever done carpentry, Johnny?"

"Never, Lee," he said. "I'm stictly an unemployed plumber, and a damn good one too."

Then proceeding to explain he would fix any leak or pipe for half the cost, because Leland Sr. was his friend, though before he could finish, the father had the man convinced, the thing he could do best, was to march up to the attic and put up the plasterboard, which had been sitting in a corner up there for two years.

"You're just the man for this job, Johnny. I know you can do," the father said, opening a bottle of Irish he stole from the dock, he bribed the plumber with a triple shot, and by noon the job was started, though it never was to be finished. As soon as the old man went off to work, the plumber snuck out the door, with the plasterboards hanging precariously, some nails having found a beam to sit in, and others rolling in the plasterboard for a lack of support or firmness to cling to. Next, when the father did have a carpenter over for a drink, he'd convince the man to fix a faucet in the kitchen or upstairs bathroom. "The best man to build a house is a truck driver," he'd say, believing every word he pronounced. The best person to tell you about Italians was a black man; the best person to tell you about marriage was a priest. The best person to explain an Irishman was a?

The attic sagged, fell, parts were still bare and uninsulated. Like other parts of Coole, don't upset the balance, this schizo ecology that worked in ratios of human beings to alcohol, or with the younger children, drugs. But Terry and Wolfe liked the attic, it was a place to be alone and away from their father.

Santa Claus? Wolfe thought, returning to the original conversation. Wolfe stared at Terry, he looked at Terry as though he were mad, the chances 50/50 that he was. They heard Leland below in the bathroom, shattering his image to the floor by breaking the mirror over the sink. His person fragmented along the tiles, and they hear him piecing his life together, cursing at the sharp edges in one year, the dull fractured images of another; the old man still running around the living room, like an engine for HO trains that neither boy would ever get, it was out of the question to even imagine a set of trains for Christmas; then there were the infinite dribbling voices of brothers, sisters, mother, saints in heaven and the devil right below. A scratching Bing Crosby record rolls out on the cartridge, Terry thinking about that dumb movie the nuns made them see every year, White Christmas. While Wolfe's mother Rose is wilted, she is shedding petals in the cellar next to her unwashed wash, measuring the goodness in her soul by the amounts of dirty laundry she stacks next to the dryer; Terry wonders: "Will mommy start to speak Russian, if she keeps drinking vodka." Terry then starts to work with the barbells harder and faster, his face red with rage for his father, for his mother, for himself. Then there is Oona and Sam directly below these two princes; the girls are in their head room on the second floor, it is the neatest room in the house (a merit badge for the domestic verities of dope). Terry once had a recurring nightmare about that room two weeks before last Christmas. He is thinking: Men in leather boots up to their knees are stomping through the Coole House; they are looking for fugitives, the entire family hidden in the small head room. Terry smells the stale liquor breaths, he is surrounded by Leland, the old man, mother Rose, Emmett; he is suffocated by their sweating bodies, their bodies also growing fatter, each time the father lies, Leland lies, mother Rose, no, she never lies, Emmett lies, they grow fatter, and each lied many times in the head room, except the mother Rose, who got skinnier and began to disappear from Terry, who cried out for her, momma momma! The father promised Terence a present, if he didn't scream; the father said he would take he and Wolfe to a ball park, when the men left and they were no longer fugitives. "You are my favorite son, Terry," the father said, and proceeded to grow another foot fatter. "You're the best kid I've ever known," he said to his son, and the father's chin drooped lower, fatter, more grotesque. Terry then woke, hollering in the attic, he bolted upright in his bed, hitting his head on the slanted ceiling, and fell peacefully back to sleep. He was rubbing that bump now as he spoke with Wolfe.

They heard the two girls below, and knew they were tripping. Emmett even more below, in the dining room, was arguing with the father about his marriage, the old man saying to his son, he was a rotten father, that is, Emmett, not the father himself, was a rotten father. "That's a good one," Terry said. Terry persisted, adding five pounds to each side of the barbells, his arms bursting the veins, his muscles swelling. Wolfe Tone Coole smoked a cigarette, allowing himself three a day and one can of beer, because he was in training to become the greatest baseball player that ever lived. The father and brothers had told him this, since he was in the crib, punching his stomach lightly when he was in the *bassinet*. "To harden him up for sports," Emmett said, when the mother marched into the room, she demanded to know why the baby was crying. Wolfe was not crying now, he thought —this Christmas—wasn't balling his eyes out, he'd been through a decade with this holy family's crusade, and he knew what to expect by now, that he would walk down to the living room the next morning after his father's battle with the demons the night before; he would find a tag with a drawing of a piece of holly on the right, his name scribbled by his mother there, WOLFE, he would unravel the knots, the bows, tear the paper, find his one pair of socks, the underwear, the flannel shirt, though was this, no, what he wanted, he wanted a catcher's mitt, softball and bat, fielder's glove, basketball, football helmet, cleats, shoulder pads, soccer ball, spikes, basketball net, knead's foot oil for his baseball glove, thigh pads with football pants, a rosin bag, baseball hat, stickball bat, Spalding High Bouncer, a fishing rod, was that asking too much?

Santa who?

"I guess I don't," he said.

Wolfe shrugged his shoulders, he walked through a pile of papers and books, as one might walk through a field of alfalfa, picking up an old glove that Michael used when he was a boy; Mickey Mack saved for six months to get it, too small, Wolfe thought, you couldn't keep a ball in the pocket; Wolfe picked the glove up like a dead bird found in a sunny meadow, the plasterboard chipped and peeled above him like a cloud, he said, like a gray rain cloud, but nope, Wolfe, he said, that's a dumb idea, that's a peeling ceiling face it boy; he tried to smile at his brother Terry, but he was crying, Wolfe was crying, and he didn't want Terry to see, since he had made, this last summer, the major leagues in baseball, then the town found he was too young and he had to go back to the town farm division for younger kids, he had lied about his age in order to play, and better than the older boys, he went begrudgingly, crying, but vowed he would never shed another tear as long as he lived, he wet his bed that night as usual, but the difference this time being, when Terry made fun of him for wetting the bed, he said:

"Mickey Mantle pissed in the sheets till he was sixteen years old."

In the whole round world this only one.
He's the one, the one they call
Wolfe Tone Coole, the seventh son.

If you count Aidan, the ghost of Aidan, like the Ghost of Christmas Past, he had the sense to die when he was five days old, baptized, they send him straight to heaven, the trouble being, you could do a season in Coole, plodding along the open spaces in the crowded house of junk and people, and still they may damn you to hell after the ordeal, it made you understand why the old man hated Christmas with such gusto, the old boy might have been tapped into the mystical root, that branch that availed him the world's knowledge, there is no hope for us damned, the old man saying into the face looking up at him from his beer, Terry! he says, outloud in the bar, but no, he says, Mickey Mack! he says out loud, but wrong again, Mr Fat Lee Coole, the foam on your beer gone, those bloodshot eyes looking up from your glass of beer, the eye of the storm, the eye of the father, he was horrors for weeks with the thought of his own image disturbing his sleep, Leland, Uncle Lee.

The thought in Wolfe's head, heaven for him was a fielder's glove, which he knew he wasn't going to get, he was stuck in purgatory, because they couldn't damn him yet, his baseball world he reigned over saved him, though the absence of the glove posited him in purgatory, he was hoping a great player, say Joe DiMaggio was doing a novena for Wolfe, getting a plenary indulgence so that Wolfe could move from third base to home, the grand slam coming with angel trumpets in his ear, Wolfe thought of the movie, *The Jackie Robinson Story*, that he would go out on the sandlot come this spring, like Jackie, he fielded pop flies barehanded, deftly, with the precision of Willie Mays, basketing the ball at his midsection, they'd buy him a glove, presenting him with a mitt the day the season opened with those longwinded speeches at the Little League dinner held at the American Legion Hall.

A cheap mitt to cover my hand, Wolfe thought.

Not that he needed a glove, he wanted the glove for his style, standing out there in left field with his right hand poking its fist into the pocket, bent over, his hands resting on his knees, he waits for that bum at the plate to pop a high one out to him, Wolfe'd rob him of that chance to connect with a triple or homer, W. Tone Coole snags it at the fence, throwing the ball to the second baseman to tag the runner out, the guy jumped the gun, "the bum was faked out of his jock strap," Wolfe says.

"What?" Terry says, putting down his weights to turn to his brother.

"Nothing," Wolfe said, walking to T., Wolfe faced his brother, the tears gone, he was tougher than the last time his brother Terry looked at him, Terry stronger too than the last time their glances crossed. Tough sonbitches, Terry said, faking a Southern accent he heard on the television last night, when the old man turned it off, saying, it was bad for their morale, that's the word he used, strutting into the next room like an Admiral, Wolfe looked at Terry, "is he kidding?"

"What did I hear you say, Terry?" the old man said, marching back into the room like a flat foot sailor.

"I said it," Wolfe admitted.

The old man belted T.

"It doesn't matter who said it," dear old dad said, strutting back into the next room like a petty officer. "There's no excuse for a son to talk to me like that."

"Pretty soon we'll be out of here," Terence said, they adjourned to their attic, where Terry told Wolfe what he was going to do . . .

Terry was telling Wolfe that when he grew up, he was going to be like Leland, "I'm going to work in a factory and come home at night, just sit in the cellar drinking beer and watching late movies on television," he said, his eyes getting dreamy, he drifted off, picturing how good it was going to be, no more school, no more girls coming over to bother him, they used to come by every day, as many as six of them, with candy and presents for T., he thought they were silly, "smoking a pack a day," he said, soaking Wolfe in his fantasy, "a six pack under my arm, I'm going to own a convertible that I'll install a telephone in, so daddy can't rip it out when he gets drunk," that was the old man's hobby, to rip the phone out of the wall about once every two weeks, this happened after he got home those nights when he called from the pier and the line was busy, because one of the girls was talking with a boyfriend, the mother called up the phone company to send a repairman, the guy shows, the same as the week before, she tells him, "the dog chewed the wire again," the guy smiling, as he looked at the unbitten rip near the socket in the wall, he fixed it, saying, "I'll see you in a couple of weeks, Mrs. Coole . . ."

"Then I can play my guitar without anybody bothering me about it," Terry said, because they complained when he practiced in Coole.

"I'm going to be the greatest baseball player that ever lived," Wolfe said, "that's all I want."

"Maybe you can write a book about it someday, a baseball book," but Wolfe shook his head no, he said he was just going to play the game, nothing else.

"I'm going to bowl twice a week too," Terry said, "Maybe I'll get a girlfriend and live with her like Michael does, but never get married, ick, never," he says, making a sour face.

T. said the last thing with a conviction that made you realize he wasn't kidding.

"I don't want anyone to grow up like this," he said.

"Me either," Wolfe said, wrestling his brother off the bed, they were fighting playfully.

"What's going on up there? What are you breaking now?"

Smiling, knowing that the old man was getting too fat to make it up the stairs, they continued bunking into their furniture, they were ignoring him.

"When you come down, Terry, I'm going to whack you good," but that was the price of knowing Wolfe, Terry thought, it didn't matter who was doing it, Terry was to blame.

The old man never hit Wolfe, he was afraid of the name, that he really believed his youngest son was going to be great, where all the others failed, he didn't want Wolfe being interviewed after playing a great game, "I owe what I've done to my family," the young star said, "all except my father who ruined my pitching arm when he twisted it one day for making too much noise," the fans roar, the voices of his frenetic family a drop in the bucket of, but the old man was smart, he didn't want anything like that to happen with the Wolfe, even his name rang of a .350 batting average and the most valuable player in the league.

"It was my father, who used to come home from work tired, he'd stand out there in the yard, feeding me a pepper game off a thirty-two inch bat, it was him that made me what I am."

What did it matter what a son said who played the guitar and had a lot of girlfriends.

"This next song is dedicated to my father, it's called 'No Good Blues for his Brown Shoes,'" Terry Coole said to his audience at the Fillmore.

Or a son who wrote books:

"My father, and using the word loosely, he was . . ."

A son who had shock treatment was useless but you couldn't throw him out, he may come back to kill you.

A son who leaves his wife Christmas day was no son worth talking about.

A daughter who was a beautician, a son and daughter who were painters, a third daughter who, too soon to tell with Deirdre, and one girl is enough, but a baseball player, he could talk to the boys on the dock about that.

"See the news today, Wolfe Tone Coole is leading the league in homers again, anytime you need a pass to Shea, I'll just call up my kid to reserve us a few seats."

Like the time Leland had a friend playing on the New York Jets, the old man didn't want to drive the kids to meet the guy in a warm up practice, but he loads them in the car, Terry, Wolfe, Leland, a few other kids on the block, they get there, and none of them can talk to the guy because the old man has monopolized the day, like he was a groupie, asking for his autograph, what does he weigh, the guy turns to Leland, "who is this guy?"

Leland smiled at his friend.

"My father . . ."

So what happened as a result of this fatherly love, whenever Wolfe did a bad thing, Terry got hit, no matter where he was when the crime occurred.

"I may be able to beat him sooner than I think," Terry said to Wolfe, as they wrestled around the room of the attic.

"I'm going to come up there and spank you, Terry," the old man said.

"Just try it, Fatso," he yelled.

"What did I hear you say?"

He was smiling at Wolfe.

"You heard me, Fatso, I'm going to get you. If you don't stop making that noise, I'm going to come down to get you."

The old man was looking around for an ally.

"What are they smoking up there, someone get your mother."

"Better keep quiet, Fats."

The old man's face looked lobstery.

"You wait, no presents for you tomorrow."

Terry didn't care.

"Keep your underwear, socks and flannel shirt, I don't need them anyhow."

"I'll have to take that bowling ball back."

Terry looked at Wolfe stunned.

He whispered to him.

"You think he got me one?"

Wolfe, who found the presents a few days earlier, shook his head, no, it was bluff, he said.

"Stick it up your you-know-where, daddy," he said, laughing, he and Wolfe started to wrestle again.

"Get your mother," the old man called downstairs, he had lost one of his strongholds, the right to abuse Terry, it seemed that after thirty years of marriage he was losing the war, the revolution was near, his slaves were about to revolt, it would go down in history as The Christmas Uprising, a band of two insurgents camped in the hills of the attic, held out for three weeks, eating their mattresses for food, they staved off the ruler, Inspector Coole, until he admitted defeat, he resigned his post, Captain Terence Coole assuming the position of the house, he ordered a beefsteak and a case of beer to be brought to him in his encampment in the attic, at an interview with the reporter Mickey Mack Coole, he discussed his strategy.

"I held out for fifteen years, probably longer than any other opponent to face him. What I did, trained each day, slowly building the militia, arms like cannons, I ran four miles a day, I shadow boxed, I took his insults, let him slap me with his glove, watched him pillage my land, saw him rape my mother nightly, stood back as he whipped my sisters, and finally, that fateful Christmas, armed with my assistant, Wolfe Tone Coole, the seventh son on my side, it was hard for the old man to sustain this moral loss, we trounced him."

"How long would you estimate the battle lasted?"

Terry smoked a big cigar, he was wearing Army fatigues.

"The actual hand to hand combat lasted throughout the greater portion of Christmas Eve night, then early Christmas day, just before the tree was turned off, he retreated to the cellar for assistance from Leland, but the oldest son was too drunk to do battle, his wife was sound asleep in her quarters, his daughters in their rooms, we de-pants him first, then made him walk barefoot through the snow, he pleaded for religious asylum, so just before dawn, when we lined him up near the garage, he didn't smoke cigarettes, but we let him have one last glass of beer, that seemed to calm him, for he was hysterical, we loaded our guns, lined him up at the wall, the local priest came by to give him the last rights so he'd make it to heaven, he mumbled a few last solemn words, "I've been a good father no matter what Terry has indicted me for," we raised our guns to our shoulders, I paused, "is that all you want to say?" I asked the prisoner, but the old man muttered "I want to say that I loved my friends on the dock and I think it a shame that the guineas are taking it over," I pulled the trigger, his guts shooting over the garage, church bells rang, for a savior was born and a killer had died, the seventh son marched with me into the headquarters, we opened our presents, went outside and placed the flannel shirts, the underwear, the socks over our father's body, as he lay hunched over in the snow in our backyard, it was snowing again, so that by the time the first Catholics passed on their way to an early morning Mass, the snow had covered Inspector Coole, he looked like a snowman, his Christmas presents at his feet, the blood that dripped through looked like buttons on the snowman, we went back to the guerilla base in the attic, counting the bills in his wallet, since we stripped him of belongings before he faced the firing squad, there was enough American dollar bills (they are negotiable in our province) for a bowling ball for me and a fielder's glove for Wolfe Tone Coole, we rejoiced, for the father was gone, a son was born, and two more were going to get what they wanted for Christmas . . ."

"He is wacky," the old man says, wacky, crazy, and nutty, filled with shinanegans, boiling with carousings, there's no curb to his tongue asking questions. Terry knew about Sam, Oona, the others who took drugs, they offered him grass enough, trying it once, he said, "I laughed, then I felt dizzy, then I stared." That was all for rushes, but beer, not wine or whisky, that old cerveza fria, he talked for days with Wolfe about six packs behind shopping centers, riding in cars with older boys to the beach, make out in the back seat with older girls, share a six pack with them, he could talk brands, commercials, the foam, bubbles to this girl, she'd be staring out the window, what kind of nut is this?

Then there was the time Terry came to Michael's apartment in New York City, and he read his older brother's writing.

"This is great, do you show these to girls?"

Michael told him, yes he did.

"Does it make them horny?"

Yes it did, some of them.

"What I'm going to do is," he said, "write poems like this, work in a factory, get drunk on beer every night. I'll write poems in the cellar, then give these poems to girls, but never publish these poems, just slip these here poems in their pockets, after I kiss or fuck them."

T.'s crony Wolfe was another story, he was a jock, gung ho! Poetry, girls, he didn't want to hear from, the women he knew, which was his sister Deirdre, he beat up, liked to wrestle, because he won, but Wolfe was the baby and with all his hard talk, he was frightened, like the oldest brother, this environment assaulted him, and baseball was his out, it swooped him out of the well into the heavens, he got his rushes this way. One day a garage door slammed down on his hand, chopping off three of the fingers, it made it impossible for him to throw the ball to home plate, but he couldn't let it stop him, he developed this weird knuckling, curving, dropping, faltering pitch that no one could hit, but tonight, Christmas Eve, he was staring at the three missing fingers, really, the spaces where they used to be, he woke in the middle of last night, he'd feel one of the missing fingers itching him, then scratching, there was nothing there, he thought of music now, because Leland had shown him a record with Django Rheinhart, Wolfe said, "he's the guy that plays the music on Farmer Gray cartoons," but Lee told him, 'maybe you'll become a great guitarist like him,' explaining about the famous gypsy's fingers, Wolfe stared at the cover of the record, he was thinking how he'd look in a mustache, but not as doing *cante gitano,* he wasn't into music, he wanted the rhythm of baseball still, he thought of himself like the first baseball players, with a handlebar mustache, but being a holiday and the winter he had pushed the baseball to the rear, he was music, all sound flowed through his missing fingers, he decided, Wolfe picked up the guitar he had fooled with for the last month, his moment of glory about to shine through, he hadn't told even Terry what he was practicing for the last month, he opened the beginners' book to the song he had learned and picking up Terry's guitar, he walked into the mess below, he moved into the holocaust with the instrument he strummed, like a somnabulist, he was pale, blond, small, a repenting angel, he drifts through the ravers, the screamers, the hawkers, like an Arab boy moves among the Bedouin merchants, like a mystical athlete, mythical in his quest, his task is to quell the rage in their hearts with his lyre, Wolfe Tone Coole strums "Rudolph the Rednosed Reindeer," not well, but you could tell the melody, his relations fighting, drunk, tripped out, he caught them for a second, he had once more attained the pinnacle, they stopped, as he walked through the detritus of the living room, past the Christmas tree, he sang it now, he stopped them for a few seconds, the noise ebbing, that was all, he acted as a mute, then he sat down, the noise is high tide, tidal, typhoon, a squall, screechings, clatter . . .

Wolfe walked into the porch, putting down his guitar, he hadn't said a word to Emmett, since he had named his kid after him, Emmett walked in to explain to Wolfe, but Wolfe got up, walked out of the room, went back up into the attic, and wrote on the wall,

THERE IS ONLY
ONE
WOLFE, HE IS
THE 7TH
SON

Deirdre was writing on her wall too, she appeared oblivious to the noise that surrounded her, it was impossible to know what this little fat girl with the knotty blond, dirty blond hair thought. Her note above her bed, just below her crucifix, still the religious one, Deirdre thought of herself this minute like Saint Theresa, humble, quiet, vaguely imbued with the holy ghost, *The Diary of Anne Frank,* her favorite book, her scroll said:

I LIKE MY DADDY

She did, the explanation being, like Michael, they had camouflage at times, in his case, except for the old man, Inspector Coole, who had that mirror trick conned the father whenever he saw the third son resembling a forgotten life, his striking out at the mirror in his son, though the discerning eye could make the distinction, but other times, the good life, Michael had his camouflage, like Deirdre has, which allowed him or her to observe events unscathed, he was Michael the Archangel, people didn't see him, oh Deirdre you too honey, she looked like the neighbor's kid come over for a visit and was often treated that way, mother Rose often forgot her name . . .

"Eat your sandwich, Sam, I mean, Oona, er, Sheila, whatever your name is."

She was round, like a Little Lotta live, she was sweet, firm, but nutty, never speaking to you directly, but wandering off, fully packed, a face that walks into a building on the lower east side, a rundown block, the building dilapidated, it will be a commune, and there in the kitchen, Deirdre, making a stew for the Hell's Angels, but even that is not clear, it comes mostly from her long hair, scraggly she doesn't comb unruly, though she could wind up being, Deirdre Coole sings the blues, one night only, you baffle them baby, what's going on in your head?

She winks, sticking her hand into another stocking for candy.

"How can you steal Michael's candy, Deirdre," Terry says, "when he's in jail without a friend?"

I LIKE MY DADDY, I LIKE HIM SO MUCH

she continued to think, as Terry and the Wolfe corner her, they are the last triangle in Coole, the final command, they are off in the corner arguing, like the big people on the other side of the room, the room has a conspiratorial air, the Anarchist faction pitted against the Falangist, the old regime dragging its corpse to the grave, while the young plot the course of the new animal bred in their blood.

"I just took a piece," she says, pretending to talk like her big sisters, she realizes she has a few more years to match their charm.

"He's got to go tomorrow," the old man says to mother Rose about Emmett staying overnight.

"If this place doesn't quiet down, I'm going to start breaking heads," Leland says, emerging from the cellar, primeval, a beast aroused from the Stone Age.

"I didn't do anything, she said I had to leave," Emmett tried to explain to his mother, who was looking for where she misplaced her drink.

"What's the idea of playing my guitar?" Terry said, pulling Wolfe by the ear.

"I'm the only Wolfe," he said to Emmett, as Terry dragged the only one off to the corner to fight.

"I like my mommy too," Deirdre said, talking to herself, as she put trimmings on the tree.

"I'm not kidding," Leland said, talking to the tree.

"When I was a girl . . ." mother Rose thus spoke to her drink.

"This house is noisy as a guinea wedding," the old man said to—

"Is there a giraffe on the lawn?" Sam said to Oona, walking down the stairs, the two belles, their eyes glazed with the universe in them, they had been visiting the cosmos in their head room, coming back to the world, the lights on the tree glowed, the members of, standing around the tree, bickering, it went counter clock then.

"The only one, Emmett," Wolfe said.

"But she threw me out, Wolfe," he said to him, not hearing what his younger brother had to offer.

". . . slam upside the head . . .": Leland.

"A bum, that guy," the old man, pointing to Santa.

". . . we'd dunk for apples, but that might have been Halloween, I always get the two mixed up," mother Rose.

"His watch went like that, tock then tick, reversing itself in the spring," Sam Coole to Oona.

"A puppy dog too," Deirdre.

"Should I do it now?" Terry asked Wolfe. "Should I hit him over the head, Wolfe?"

"The greatest baseball player . . ."

"The second sundae tomorrow, Sam," she said.

"Wacky, I tell you, wacky like a bum, like a . . ."

". . . pumpkins in the chimney and Easter eggs in the stockings, I remember now," M. Rose said.

"That nutty kid, I'll put coal in his . . ."

". . . break heads, that's what, I rode freights, remember that line . . ."

"She asked me if I like the name Oscar and I had to admit it sounded awful."

"But Wolfe," Terry said to Emmett, "why call him Wolfe?" the seventh son listening to Terry defend his name.

"A barbarian, I tell you, a jackass," the old man said.

"Just kick ass . . .": Leland.

"I like my mommy and daddy too."

"Like a bum, that's what . . ."

Around the tree, bicker poll, fight, backbiting, syndicate, equivocate, cursing, blasphemies, punches, who pushed who, get your feet off my pair of underwear, Old Spice cologne, flannel underwear, he says, the old man being imaginative this season, argue, the crescendo, ratter, the house shakes with the voices rising like a moon, bright and causing people to be susceptible to madness, oh what joy tidings, pinching, pummeling, Noël, Noël, Noël, Noël, born is the King of
Is-rye-el . . .

157

CHAPTER NINE

Brothers Pat and Mike, after awhile the nostalgia grass worked on them so bad, they got on the subway at W 4th Street, took the E train to 179th Street, Jamaica, waiting out in that cold Hillside Avenue snow at the Mineola bus stop, Schenk Bus Line, they never show at night, they waited hours, freezing, when they finally decided to walk down the road for coffee, the bus pulled up, the driver looking arrogant and warm, condescending to them like they were entering his famous chalet in the Swiss Alps, if he had his way, he would have made them sit in the rear, away from the guests, but they walked back there voluntarily, sitting on the last seat, the vibration from the engine got circulation back in their bodies, they arrived in town feeling up, they marched down the block, the nostalgia grass working, even after they heard the cacophony about a block and a half away, they opened the door, walking into the theater, there were the performers, these members of the family, froze, again for that instant like they did when Wolfe walked by with his guitar, they said hello to the new additions, collectively, all nine there, they greeted the two of them here . . .

"Hi!" "It's Michael!" "Hello." "If it isn't the bard returned." "My son." "What's the bum want?" "I like my brother Michael too." "Far out!" "Look what the cat bought in."

After that intro, it was like he never left, they returned to their discussions.

"There's only one Wolfe, Emmett," Wolfe said.

"If he really lived, I'd like to kill Santa Claus tonight," Leland said to Deirdre, who winced walking away from him.

"I don't know if I like Leland," she said to a doll she found under the tree with her name on it.

"It looks like a guinea tree," the old man said to the tree.

"When I was a nurse," the mother said.

"She just told me to leave, that was all," Emmett continued to tell the old man, who wasn't listening anymore.

"The giraffe will be blue, Oona."

"   ," Oona said.

"I'm going to drink two six packs a day," Terry said to Wolfe, Wolfe said to Terry, "the best player in the league . . ."

Michael walked around the house, a ghost, he had his old invisible touch, they'd never notice him, even more so now since he had come to be quieter, reticent, he moved through the rooms, losing Pat who plopped out on the bed in Oona's room after taking a monstrous toke on her hookah, Mickey Mike careened through the rooms, looking at the hieroglyphs on the wall, the newest being Wolfe's earlier testament in the heart shape, he was cloaked in memories, the present musty with the old, his own fury was mild compared to the noise below, he wondered how he lasted till fifteen, living in this house, to run away happy through New York alone and adolescent, and what did he feel for the folks down below, not just the mother and father, but all those brothers and sisters, too many, how you expect a man to respond to that many souls, he removed his scarf, he was in the attic now, sitting down on Wolfe's bed, he got up quick, the wetness, the smell of piss, the old manuscripts piled in the corner, the vertigo set in.

The house was a museum, literally, of natural history, each inhabitant here made the center of his life a collection of things, the mother storing up children, the father collecting beer waste around his belly, the oldest son a collector of misanthropic dreams, the brother Emmett a collector of . . .

He reeled, thinking of them.

Smells assaulted him, bringing back old memories.

Michael pissed in the bathroom, looking in the bowl that had never been washed in years, one handle on the sink missing, a pliers on the porcelain to turn the sprocket for hot water, the medicine cabinet filled with rusty razors, hundreds of them, a gray-blue bathtub ring the same as when he left, the same three tiles missing on the floor, the same six missing on the wall, the piece of plaster hanging like an udder from the ceiling, it had

160

cobwebs on it, the same spider's nest that he saw ten years ago, he opened the closet door to the bathroom, remembering that he and Emmett had chopped a small hole through the bedroom on the other side, they had done it when a beautiful cousin was visiting for a week, so that if the closet door stayed open, the hole centered right on her twat when she sat down to piss.

The closet was filled, five feet high with empty aerosol cans, maybe a thousand of them, for some reason when any member used a deodorant spray, a room freshener spray, a shaving cream can, they threw it into this closet, instead of putting it in the waste paper basket below the sink, the cans were rusty, smiling like an oxidized snowman at Michael, in two years the pile would be his height, then they'd have to find a new closet to throw their aerosol bombs in, though there wasn't much space left, walking into the parents' bedroom, clothes, sheets, towels, curtains, old pants, records, magazines, piled about the room like ant hills, human insect forts, but warm, you could sink down into any heap of garbage, just pick any room, cozy fertile bins where memory never ceased, where fantasy ruled, he had come once again to wonderland.

But this time Mickey Mack Coole is a visit, not even the visitor, he is the action of a person come to find that the seeds of his imagination took their powers from these musty rooms, a seven room house fogged with a million crack ups, a clan of visionaries here, there wasn't a need for acid, the hallucinations abounded, the wall paper scraped and written on, *Deirdre loves Fatty Kelly,* you know Wolfe had to do that to tick her off, it lay resting above her bed like an epitaph, these folk were from the slums, the Coole tribe, but they didn't have their ghetto no more, they had to make a private shitheap within the heart of a suburban area, working as antibodies to the cancer around them, though the community thought them the malignancy, the old man got a new citation from the town government once a month, rundown house, improper shingles on roof, broken windows, garage in condemnable shape, hedges too high, litter obstructing pedestrian traffic that passed his door, they needed a subway, the Cooles, a place to hang out, scribbling their graffiti on the walls, instead they did it on the walls of their castle, their Alamo—hear the toilet backing up—which means they haven't repaired that particular plumbing difficulty since Michael lived here ten years ago, or else the old man hired a baker to fix the pipes, wrapping a cruller around the severed threads on the fittings, Mackool took off the porcelain lid, put his hand in the tank behind the bowl, pulled the plunger by hand so that the well fills with water, he's floating up to his attic again, this time he sits on Terry's bed . . .

"All right, you bum, out of bed," the old man punching him in the stomach, Mickey Mike rolls over and dad lets fly with one in his kidney, don't have a chance to open his eyes, find out what the charges are this time, but Sunday morning, it has to be a religious felony, ten to, the last mass going on at one o'clock, "what's this about you smoking in the attic?" punch punch, punch, it was the muggy attic where Mackool had come to rest in, Leland getting out of the nut ward in Philly, he'd been discharged from the Army, they gave him the room on the porch, it was too damp there anyway, the attic suited Michael fine, so ten to, the father's giving these religious rabbit punches, asking the son why he smoked in the attic last night, another punch, liberally shot into the nape like a bad judo chop, the boy is out of the bed going All Right All Right, what's the matter this time, but this time, like all the others, he's never sure what he's being hit for, it's arbitrary, done solely, it seems, so that the father doesn't break character, let his son see that he's got a heart, he never did.

Uncle Leland Sr., the dad, Inspector Coole was a maniac.

Fat as the walrus, he's boring again with, "a disgrace to your mother," his false teeth in a jar in the bathroom, his mouth shrivels like a Dick Tracy criminal as he speaks, the words jumbled like he had a rubber ball there, talking to his son from behind the ball, his words come out fast, incoherent, he won't leave Michael for a minute to dream of the splendor, the secret harmony of all men.

"Your poor mother, what she has to put up with!"

As though he cared, in five minutes when the bars opened, he'd be around the corner downing his first fifteen cent beer at fifteen seconds past the hour, "here's looking at you, Lee," the bartender said, as Michael and Pat and Emmett stood outside the candy store, one brother each week going into the Mass and when he came out, they went home, one told them what the sermon was about, ("who gave it?") when the mother asked, Emmett'd say:

"Father O'Brien, he talked about the sixth commandment," sitting down to have bacon and eggs, she'd be pleased that her sons saved their souls for another Sunday.

Saturday nights were different.

"Put your dear mother on," the old man said, talking to Oona on the telephone, he was in the bag, "I'm sleeping on the ship tonight, getting a little overtime for the kids, dear."

For the kids, that phrase reverberating through their head like a hydraulic drill.

***   ***   ***   ***   ***   ***   ***

My father promises to take Pat to a ball game, he doesn't he forgets.

He tells Oona, he's going to buy her a bicycle, this goes on for five years, the day he gets it, he wants to ride it first, he's circling the block, he hits sand, the bike turns out from under him, his face scrapes along the pavement, his arm cracks, the bike smashes up against a tree.

The cast is on his arm for a month.

He says:

"I got a friend who's an electrician, he's a whiz fixing bikes, I'll call him the next chance I get."

Rusted, still in the garage, the bike sits, Emmett rides it up the side of the house, it has neither tires nor spokes, just the frame cruising along the rooftop, Emmett signals for a right turn, but soars into the sky.

The next thing, the father is knocking on the door of the bar, it is about three in the morning, Terry couldn't stand up, he's pulling him off the stool, "he's only fifteen," he said to Whitey, the bartender, who is passed out still in his bloody mary, he looked up, bug eyed, saying, "draftcard, he . . . twenty-five years old, veteran . . ." then blanked out, the old man pulling Terry off the stool, the father has his shirt collar wringing in hand, choking, Terence is turning blue, the father hitting across the face with a wet hand, he'll have them closed for this, he says, Terry's legs not working, he drags the son through the sawdust, a lifeless object that the father owns that he wants to beat the shit out of, because he had a bad day on the docks, but many years before, Patrick who was seventeen, he's worried the old man is going to blow his scene, he runs after the father, pulling him by the free arm, it was snowing, the air pinching not Terry's face, for he had changed earlier into Mickey Mack, into soberness, punches, the father, going numb all over his son's body, two more in the stomach, Leland throws up on his overcoat, they have a tug of war with Emmett's arms, they seem to rip out the sockets, blood covering the snow, red and white, an almost patriot, Wolfe tastes snowflakes on his tongue, wanting to write a poem about the sensation, numb, the cold air is sobering, they realize who their assassin is, it is the old man.

Immediate.

The sons in imagined son break away from him, pushing snow on the old man, the six in one runs down the block, an extra son getting up, punching the father in the face, his nose is bleeding, the seventh is running after his brother a block away, the old man a block behind him, looped, stopped short turning quickly, the eighth son almost runs into the six in one, "let's get him," they storm after Inspector Coole, who sees them rampaging toward him, he is covered with snow, puke, blood, sweat from running, his eyes with the look of a captured animal, he about faces, the twelve sons of seven running for about five minutes, they collapse at the bus depot, choking on coffee they drink to sober up, the fourteenth son continues the chase to get the old man, because the old man once brought him home to his mother, telling her, her son ran around the neighborhood ringing doorbells, the nuisance, he says, a crazy kid.

Particularly at Christmas, mother came from the better part . . . The rest of the family, furies in the kitchen, the old man . . . never, like Irish momma . . . little bundles of clothes for the children . . . filthy tired, bourbon . . . There are 300 pounds . . . I looked at him confused . . . "Our aunts, man, the furnace . . . of being fanatic more than any other Brooklyn . . . The Rangers pulled a game in the last three; Coole . . . this is going to be my second fudge sundae . . . Midnight? (The little lady, the newly acquired wife, she was a pickle . . . (I step in shit all the time . . . As I said, Emmett wasn't always another, clear & loud . . . alternating the name of address to, "this was the day that Leland fell out . . . not necessarily me, with his friend, who he hasn't seen in a holiday . . . for no reason yesterday. There hasn't been a night in the last two weeks when he didn't come home rocky, she said, I said, eating, all the candy & . . .

The attic smothered Michael, he was lying across the bed, trying to block out the commotion below, the old haunting children's hour, he was sweating, trying to bury the people he grew up with in a folder for history, it wasn't working, he couldn't get out of their Coole skin, he was buried next to him, to her, to them.

Whenever he tells them the number, visit ever, whenever, Michael never . . . "fuck of all time," Pat whispered . . . a slave approve of . . . not even doing it properly, that everyone loves, & approves, she . . . The porch, where he slept, midway the wine of the family of seven plus, an older . . . what's wrong with our house. I found the house about two feet tall, breathing my life into every room & person hooked to those rooms, I looked at the attic, carved of soap, I said hello to the old man the young man the man in the middle, whittling . . . King Midas of Shit . . . drunk, on her ear from a new bottle of children . . . smallest, but the bright public john in a bus depot, folded out: dumb old face, played by every other brother or) . . . Thirty years of marriage, she probably longer than any other arms like cannons, I ran four miles a day, bored. At the cover of the old record, the girls, Django, cante gitano . . .

Obscenely pregnant. Obscene. Pregnant.

The boy shook him awake, telling him to calm down, take this, he took it, passing out in the attic, sleeping, it was dreamless.

***　　***　　***　　***　　***　　***　　***

The kids were a hopeless baseball team of a basketball team with four subs, there was ten, no, nine, shit, he honestly forgets, really, but nine now, because the ghost of Oliver, what would he be chewing on, the sofa for pleasure, blond or black Irish, perhaps not even Irish at all, a bold Italian on the dock, he'd grow up to make the old man say, "The damn son Oliver is taking over the dock and my own wife has to serve me meatballs." They are never sure whether to count him in or out, though "he had a soul and is in heaven now," mother Rose says to the other kiddies when they ask, they say, if he were born in the same hospital as the others, maybe he would have lived, maybe she says, though they forget that Mickey Mack was born in Washington D.C., the only citizen outside Brooklyn to survive, which means in all, they were one short of a football squad, Oliver being the vanishing wing back, ten kiddies, except the entire count would be close to fourteen if you count miscarriages, Sam used to think of strollers with white tires and a blue hood, when mother looked pale she was saying to her husband at the table, "miscarriage . . ."

"Now calm down, dear, you've had a hard day."
"Call me Rose, goddamn it!"
Reeling.
She knew she hadn't done a blessed thing in weeks.
"You've been doing too much, take it easy, honey."
As though that word, the Rose upon the rood of time, would turn his beer fat to stone.

My love is like a red, red, honey

A sweetheart is a sweetheart is a sweet . . .

There is a dear in Spanish Harlem

"But sweetheart . . ."
"You know my name, stupid!"
She never talked like that, Terry and Wolfe smiled, but were astonished at her showing, they were glad the old man was going through changes.

168

"Suga . . ." He didn't get the words out, she hit him across the face with a Christmas ball.

His lip was bleeding.

He was half frantic with fear, half delighted by the attack, Leland screamed, his turn now, his lungs burst through the room.

"I knew it, she was always like that underneath all her niceness! There's no excuse for this!"

Emmett was holding the father, Deirdre crying, Pat was passed out in the head room, Oona and Sam staring at the blood as it ran down his face, it was changing colors, it was green with tiny feet glowing like pieces of glass along his chin, he looked like a sparrow with his long nose, his black eyes focused nowhere particular in dumb amazement, the blood flowing, Inspector Coole was bleeding.

"Call me Rose, that's all I want," she said.

He wouldn't do it.

There were no more babies to produce in her, fertility was everything, there were no more guineas around to ruin his supper, they just wanted him to say her name, to call out that word like she was his flower, not poetically, Terry wanted his old man to say it, Rose, upon the lips like a romance, but not corny, just to utter her name, soft, to say it like Aunt Augusta used to say Mickey Mack Coole, properly then, as though he finally knew her as the Queen, she was a woman who believed in all the old, what? He couldn't think of the word. She was a lonely saint surrounded by Satans, say her name, Sam was in the living room, nine of the children standing around the father, the mother Rose was waiting, her lips moved so that you could see one chipped front tooth, the old man's face was rubbery, he stared at the young Frankensteins around him, half of them staring at the floor, covered with debris of opened presents, wrapping paper for presents still to be wrapped, the seventh son was counting to seven on his seven fingers, he wanted him to say her name when he reached the first stub in his hand, Michael heard blubber rolling up in his brother Leland's chest, he was waiting for him to say it or not say it, it didn't matter, he wanted quiet, a drink maybe afterward with the old man in a bar, Emmett fidgeted, Deirdre played with the hem of her dress, Oona and Sam were holding on to each other, they didn't want a bummer, Patrick standing next to Michael, sleep had creased his face, Wolfe and Terry stood next to each other, they were caught tightly in their bodies, waiting, say her name you bastard, Terry thought, she was the flower, their momma, they were waiting, she looked at him again, her eyes hardened by menopause, her face cracked with wrinkles, the gray hair frizzy, uncombed, she wore sneakers with holes in the toes, a cotton dress with the armpits ripped, shredded, frustration, old age, this love in front of her, dumb, blind, devoted love, she thought.

"Say my name, Lee," she pleaded.

Inspector Coole looked around the room for assistance, he was alone.

He cried, his round belly shaking as his face contorted, his lip sucking into him, his chin began to move forward, folded, then moved forward again, the lower lip moving outward. He had lost his excuses.

An Afterword

Long Island is a fish-shaped chunk of land off another chunk of
land, Manhattan, which, as they say, is separated from America
by the Hudson River. We could carry on another geographical
parallel in regard to Ireland, with England stuck in the middle,
on the way to Europe, but this lesson has another purpose: to
hint at the basic movement of *Season at Coole*. The first move
was from Ireland to America (Brooklyn, in the case of the Coole
family); the second was from Brooklyn to the Island, Long
Island; and the third is when the kids go back to the City,
Manhattan:

> ...this scroungy house the family dwells in on Long Island,
> Irish beggars surrounded by the tacky elegance of newly
> rich, almost rich, and the rich.

There is, of course, that other Irish-American writer, F. Scott
Fitzgerald, who has written about the Island in *The Great
Gatsby,* and between them they have pretty much indicated the
shape of that place, a place with a shifting coastline and the
overwhelming feeling that once upon a time people tried to build
something but the plans got lost, got stolen, maybe there never
were any. Of course, Fitzgerald was writing about dreams and
people possessed of a dream, and the same can be said of
Michael Stephens: *Season at Coole* is a dream without any of the
messy, sentimental trappings of a usually recounted dream: the
other word for dream being vision.

Michael Stephens is an Irish-American writer. I do not mean this
as an insult or as a way to limit his appeal. *Season at Coole* is ap-
pearing in a Polish translation in Cracow, but then some people
have said that Poland is the Ireland of Eastern Europe, the same
abused history, the same emigration, the same religion, for the
most part, the same peculiar relationship between Pole and
Polish-American as between Irish and Irish-American. I shall
not rehearse that history of misunderstanding, envy, friendship,

172

lust, and dream, the frustrated dream of the father, Leland Coole, Sr., that "he would one day become the American ambassador to Ireland." Now, that is a strange dream, one still common when I was growing up on Long Island, in Patchogue, born in Brooklyn, 1944, moved to the Island, 1946... and what would Lady Gregory make of the Coole family, surely named after Coole Park and Yeats?

To grow up on Long Island, a place more famous for the rock and roll it has produced, if thought is given to what has been produced on Long Island other than Long Island potatoes, Long Island ducks, Blue Point oysters. Those are the old-line exports; now we have Lou Reed and the Blue Oyster Cult. *Out there on the Island,* where to go into the City is to be ripped off, to have experiences, and to betray the dream of the parents who made the big move, who sacrificed for the kids so that they could live on the Island, away from the City, and to remember that all great literature is the celebration of the local even if

>these folks were from the slums, the Coole tribe, but they didn't have their ghetto no more, they had to make a private shitheap within the heart of a suburban area, working as antibodies to the cancer around them.

Season at Coole is words. None of that dreary plot of complication, resolution, none of that introducing of characters, have a chat, exit characters from room. *Season at Coole* is words, words assigned to names, as we do in memory. The novel exists in the literary world inhabited by the books of Beckett, Céline, Malaparte, Kerouac, Juan Carlos Onetti.

As I write this, *Season at Coole* was published originally twelve years ago and died for all the usual drab, dumb reasons, including the book's editor dropping dead playing tennis the week the book came out, dead of the WASP'S revenge, tennis, but of course the book is and remains alive, requiring no footnotes as much of the fiction published even five years ago would require,

173

that sort of fiction supposedly rooted in the "real world." The ultimate compliment to a book like *Season at Coole:* it is totally unavailable in the used bookshops.

I read *Season at Coole* as a confirmation of my own experience, of the worth of my own experience. Because of the clarity of Stephens's vision I was able to see my own experience more fully, to see the similarities, to see the differences, possibly because truth resides in the rescued details. Anybody can work up a grand scheme, a major novel, a sizzling exposé of the wonderful and powerful. I read the newspapers for such fictions. With Stephens I am taken right into the centrality of my nervous system and am allowed again to feel, to know, to taste the sour ash of:

> then my mother had a maid
> I don't want anyone to grow up like this
> flannel shirts
> for the kids
> the damn guineas on the docks
> a champ at funerals, he missed his calling

"Hello, Coole residence"—that ran me right back to my mother telling me after I answered the phone, "Hello, McGonigle residence," after hearing when I was over at the Zimmermanns' (the old man owned a company that raised money for the archdiocese), "Hello, Zimmermann residence." Anyway, my mother saying, we don't answer the phone that way, it's pretentious and this isn't a doctor's office. This was in Patchogue, an hour and something from Mineola, more or less where the Christmas season is being undergone by the Coole family, with reports of a son in the loony bin. But you know all of this, having read the book, and never has the horror of Christmas been better illuminated with the fear of trees catching fire, the house burning down with *all* the presents inside, or as I remember once visiting a friend whose tree had lost all its needles before the end